OUT OF C

"Okay, boy," Kerry whispered nervously to Magician as she tightened his girth. The horse unexpectedly laid his ears back and tried to nip at her arm. For a second Kerry hesitated before putting her foot in the stirrup.

Maybe he's as nervous as I am, Kerry thought to herself as she swung her leg over his back and settled herself in the saddle.

That was the last sensible thought she had. As soon as Magician felt her weight on his back, he went crazy. With an angry squeal, the big, black horse erupted in a frenzy and reared up in the air, his forelegs flailing wildly in front of him.

As she hung on to his back for dear life, Kerry saw her precious screen test disappear in a puff of smoke before her panic-stricken eyes.

BEST FRIENDS

RACING FOR THE STARS

BY MAGGIE DANA

ILLUSTRATIONS BY DONNA RUFF

Troll Associates

Library of Congress Cataloging in Publication Data

Dana, Maggie.
    Racing for the stars.

    (Best Friends; #3)
    Summary: Determined to earn money to buy her
own horse, Kerry tries out for a part in a film
to be made at the Timber Ridge Riding Stables
where she lives with her friend Holly and her mother.
    [1. Horses—Fiction] I. Ruff, Donna, ill.
II. Title. III. Series: Best friends (Mahwah,
N.J.); #3.
PZ7.D194Rac   1988   [Fic]   87-16246
ISBN 0-8167-1195-X (lib. bdg.)
ISBN 0-8167-1196-8 (pbk.)

A TROLL BOOK, published by Troll Associates,
Mahwah, NJ 07430

Printed in the United States of America.

10 9 8 7 6 5 4 3 2 1

To the memory of William M. Pike

BEST FRIENDS

RACING FOR THE STARS

Chapter One

"Holly, that looked *great*!"

Kerry Logan cheered as her friend took her big, black horse over the small practice jump in the middle of the outside riding ring. The jump was only two feet high, and Magician, the horse, probably thought it was an insult to his jumping ability to have to bother with something so small and puny. Nonetheless, the girl on the horse looked triumphant.

With her long, blond hair flying out behind her from beneath her hard hat, Holly Chapman reined the horse in and trotted back toward Kerry, patting his neck and grinning happily.

Kerry grinned back. She knew exactly what was going through Holly's mind. She could read her friend like a book, and she could almost hear her saying, "That was nothing—you ought to see what I *used* to jump." But Kerry also knew how thrilled Holly was about being well enough to jump again. The girl had spent the past two years confined to a wheelchair, and it was nothing short of a miracle that she was actually walking *and* riding again.

"Do you want to ride him?" Holly asked. Her bright blue eyes were flashing with excitement, and she had streaks of mud across her face where she'd wiped the sweat away.

"Yeah. You sure you've had enough?"

"I'm beat," Holly said as she dropped the reins. She'd been riding for over an hour and was really feeling the strain in her legs. Muscles that hadn't been used in over two years were now screaming for mercy, but she didn't care. She *welcomed* the pain. It was a thrill for her to be able to feel *anything* in her legs— so even pain felt good.

Kerry took hold of Magician's reins with one hand, and with her free one helped Holly as she awkwardly slid off his back. She landed hard on the ground, and her legs crumpled beneath her.

"You okay?" Kerry asked.

Holly laughed. "I'm stiff, sore, and I hurt all over, but it feels wonderful." She reached up and grabbed Kerry's outstretched hand, and lurched clumsily to her feet.

"Think you'll be ready for the next Olympics?" Kerry teased affectionately.

"Sure." Holly grinned at her friend's absurd question. "But maybe I'd better check with Mom first, huh?"

They both laughed. Holly's mother, Liz Chapman, was the riding instructor and manager at Timber Ridge Stables. Until two years ago, Holly had ridden all her life, taught by her mother, who had once been a serious contender for the U.S. Olympic Equestrian Team. Then came the accident. A car accident had killed Holly's father and left her emotionally scarred and unable to walk. She'd only recently gotten out of the wheelchair. And although she still walked stiffly and had to use two walking canes, she was back in the saddle and riding her horse again.

"Take him over the whole course," Holly suggested as Kerry put her foot in the stirrup and swung herself over Magician's back. "I love watching you jump."

Kerry grinned and steered the magnificent black horse toward the parallel bars. As he soared over the jump, Kerry leaned forward into his flying mane, thinking how lucky she was. Riding Magician and living at Timber Ridge with Holly and her mother, Liz, were the best things that had ever happened to her. At the beginning of the summer, she'd been hired by Liz as a companion for Holly, and now Holly was her best friend.

Still thinking about Holly, Kerry cantered around the corner of the ring. Suddenly her good mood vanished. Another horse and rider had just appeared: It was Whitney Myers on her horse, Astronaut. She frowned and slowed Magician down to a trot. "Why does she always have to turn up when we're using the ring?" she said to Holly.

"I don't know. Maybe she's psychic."

"Or a witch," Kerry muttered.

Holly smothered a giggle and looked out of the

corner of her eye as Whitney and Astronaut trotted down the far side of the ring. As usual, Whitney was perfectly dressed in light tan riding breeches, a brilliantly white shirt, and highly polished black boots. Her horse was groomed to perfection, and his dark bay coat gleamed softly in the bright sunlight.

"I wonder who she got to clean him for her *this* time?" Kerry said in a low voice. It was an old joke. Whitney hated any kind of dirty work and always managed to find someone else to groom her horse, or clean his stall. Kerry stared at the new arrival as Whitney trotted past them. "I wonder what's going on? You know Whitney never rides without an audience."

"Look over there," Holly whispered urgently.

"Where?"

"Coming out of the barn."

Kerry looked. She recognized the woman immediately. It was Whitney's mother. But the man with her was a stranger; she'd never seen him around Timber Ridge before. As the couple got closer, Kerry could see the man's face more clearly and saw he had a beard. "I know who that is!" she exclaimed. "That must be Giles Ballantine. Your mother's description of him fits to a T."

Liz had given the girls a very colorful description of the famous movie producer, who also owned a big bay horse named Buccaneer. Buccaneer had been sent to the stables earlier that summer so that Liz Chapman could train him. But when Liz had injured her ankle, Kerry ended up doing most of Buccaneer's training herself.

"Let's put Magician in the barn," Kerry said under her breath as Mrs. Myers and Giles Ballantine reached the edge of the riding ring. "Then we can come out and watch Whitney showing off!"

Holly stifled another burst of laughter. She bent down, picked up her two walking canes, and stumbled out of the ring as fast as she could behind Kerry and the horse.

"Hurry up, you two," Liz Chapman called with a smile as the two girls led Magician into the barn. "Giles Ballantine is here, and I want Kerry to ride Buccaneer. He's very eager to see how his horse is doing."

"Did he say anything about the movie?" Holly asked hopefully. Ever since her mother had announced that Giles Ballantine was planning to use the Timber Ridge stables for a location shot in one of his upcoming film projects, the whole place had been buzzing with excitement.

"Well, actually, he did say something about it," Liz replied as she went into the tackroom to check on some equipment.

"What, Mom?" Holly was almost whining. "What did he say?"

"Well, apparently the star of his new movie is a young girl, so they may need a young rider to do some riding for her," Liz said.

"You mean like a stunt double."

"That's right. Only it won't be anything too dangerous. Giles is going to have a tryout here at the stables, and whoever is chosen will be paid—I believe Giles said five hundred dollars. Now go tell Kerry

5

that Giles wants to see her ride Buccaneer."

Holly was gone before her mother finished the sentence. She was bursting to tell Kerry the news. When she reached Magician's stall, Kerry had just finished brushing him off. "Better hurry up. Mom wants you to ride Buccaneer for Mr. Ballantine. And wait till you hear the news! Mr. Ballantine is looking for a young rider to ride in his movie as a double for the star. And it pays five hundred dollars! Isn't that great? You've got to try out!"

Kerry didn't say a word. A million thoughts came rushing into her head. But they all resolved themselves into one idea. If she were the one chosen to ride in the film, she'd have five hundred dollars. And if she had five hundred dollars, she knew just what she'd do with it. Buy herself a horse.

Kerry patted Magician's nose and, without missing a beat, swung into the next stall. "Hi, fella," she said happily to the dark bay horse inside.

Buccaneer whinnied softly and nuzzled her pocket.

"Guess what *he* wants," Holly teased.

Kerry rummaged around in her pocket and pulled out a crumpled packet of M&M candies. "Here you are," she said fondly to the horse.

Buccaneer gently sniffed at her outstretched hand, then greedily gobbled down the treat. Kerry laughed and patted his well-muscled shoulder.

"That horse is going to get cavities," Holly said with a laugh.

Buccaneer eagerly poked around her pockets, hoping for more. He had quickly established himself as one of the barn's favorite horses because of his unusual taste in food. When all the kids had discovered that he preferred M&M's to carrots, they fought over whose turn it was to feed him, and he was in danger of becoming spoiled.

"I wonder how long Mr. Ballantine's going to leave him with us?" Holly said as Kerry slung the saddle over the horse's back and tightened up the girth.

Kerry shrugged. She didn't want to think about it. In the few weeks that she'd been responsible for the horse's training, she'd become very fond of him and hated the thought of him leaving.

Kerry led the horse to the riding ring and felt the tension rising inside her. Liz was already out there, talking to Mrs. Myers and Giles Ballantine. Whitney was still in the ring, riding Astronaut over the jumping course and showing off for the famous visitor.

"Look at Whitney!" Holly's voice said behind her. "She must know about the part in the movie. No wonder she's putting on such a show."

Kerry glanced toward horse and rider, and grinned. She nodded at Holly. Whitney was obviously so intent on impressing Giles Ballantine that she didn't realize she was cantering on the wrong lead. Astronaut stumbled as they came to the corner and almost lost his balance. His rider's foolish-looking smile vanished as she fought to remain on his back.

"That'll teach her," Holly muttered. "I bet she's only grinning like that to show him her perfect white teeth. She probably figures she's got the part automatically."

"Well, her parents are friends of Mr. Ballantine's," Kerry reminded Holly.

7

"Don't jump the parallel bars, Whitney." Liz's voice rang out loudly.

Kerry looked into the ring again. Sure enough, Whitney was determined to show off. The jump that Liz had referred to was set at almost four feet, and it had an enormous spread to it. Kerry had been jumping Magician over it earlier, and she knew Whitney had seen her. She held her breath as the girl purposely ignored her riding instructor's words. Whitney flicked her crop across Astronaut's rump and pushed him toward the red and white jump.

"Whitney, I said—" Liz's angry words were cut off as the girl on the horse thundered forward. It was too late. There was no way she could stop him now.

Astronaut put in one extra short stride before the takeoff, and Whitney was thrown off balance. She jerked at his mouth as he took off so she didn't lean forward soon enough. Astronaut tried his best to clear the fence, but his rider's panic-stricken movements stopped him from succeeding. Whitney lost a stirrup and lurched violently to one side. As the horse landed on the other side of the jump amid the crashing poles, she fell off.

"Gee, that was really something, wasn't it?" Holly said sarcastically as both Liz and Mrs. Myers ran toward the fallen rider. Giles Ballantine stayed at the fence, his attention focused on Buccaneer rather than the disaster in the middle of the ring.

Kerry could hear Liz scolding Whitney as Mrs. Myers anxiously fretted and fussed over her daughter. Whitney didn't seem to be hurt; just angry, from

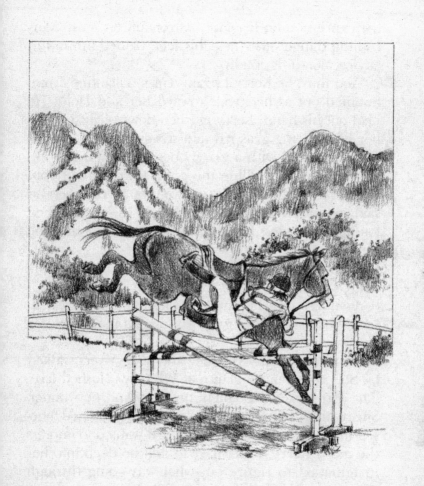

the expression on her face. Astronaut, his loose reins trailing dangerously near his feet, trotted around in circles, neighing loudly.

"You must be Kerry Logan," Giles Ballantine's voice boomed out as he strode toward her and Holly. He held out his hand. Kerry reached down shyly and felt her hand being grasped in a strong grip. It felt like shaking hands with a grizzly bear. She smiled.

"Liz has been telling me good things about you, young lady," Giles Ballantine went on. "And she also said you're feeding my horse M and M's!" He laughed loudly and patted Buccaneer's neck. "Just don't spoil him too much, okay?"

"I won't," Kerry promised, wishing she had the nerve to ask him about the movie.

As if reading her mind, Giles Ballantine asked, "Are you one of the girls who are going to try for the part in my film?"

Kerry nodded as Whitney and Mrs. Myers walked by. She stole a quick glance at Whitney's flushed face. The girl looked absolutely furious. And no wonder. She'd just disobeyed orders and embarrassed herself in front of the one person she'd wanted to impress the most. Kerry didn't have to dig too deep into her imagination to figure out what was going through Whitney's mind at that very moment.

She tore her gaze away from Whitney's angry face and tried to concentrate on making Buccaneer look good for his owner. The big bay horse behaved himself perfectly, and Giles Ballantine was all smiles when Kerry finished her ride.

"He looks like a different horse!" the movie pro-

10

ducer exclaimed as he patted Buccaneer's neck. "You've done wonders with him."

Kerry smiled shyly, but her pleasure at Giles Ballantine's praise was spoiled by the expression on Whitney's face. She knew in an instant that until Mr. Ballantine chose the rider for his film, she and Whitney would be locked in a rivalry that would only end when the winner was announced.

After she had put the horse back in his stall and rubbed him down, she joined Holly in Liz's office.

"Are you going to ride Buccaneer in the screen test, or would you like Magician?" Holly asked.

"You're definitely not going to try for it, huh?"

Holly shook her head sadly. "Mom would never let me. And I guess she's right. I mean, I'd be awful stupid to take a risk doing this and mess up my chances for the next team event."

"I'd love to ride Magician, then," Kerry said. Much as she enjoyed riding Buccaneer, he was still unpredictable and she really wanted to do well in the screen test. With Magician she knew she'd have a better chance for success.

Kerry glanced at the notice board on the wall. Holly's remark about the next team riding competition had brought back another worry. Kerry didn't know how long she would remain at Timber Ridge. Her father was still away on business in the Middle East, and she didn't know when he was coming home.

The list of riding team members had grown. There had been only four riders when Kerry first arrived. Now there were six, but only five horses. Quickly she scanned the list:

Whitney Myers	Astronaut
Robin Lovell	Tally Ho
Jennifer McKenna	Prince
Susan Armstrong	Tara
Holly Chapman	Magician
Kerry Logan	—

Kerry was determined to do something about the blank space beside her name, and Giles Ballantine's movie was the answer!

"Are you going to ride in the Winchester horse show?" Kerry asked, tearing her eyes away from the notice board.

Holly grinned happily. "You bet! Mom says I'll be strong enough by then. Hey, did she tell you? They've changed the date to the last weekend in August."

Kerry's heart sank. There was no way Buccaneer would still be at the barn by then. Mr. Ballantine was planning on taking him away by mid-August. She felt bitterly disappointed. She'd been hoping that both she and the candy-loving horse could compete together with the riding team at least once before they both left for who knows where.

"Kerry, what's wrong? You look awful."

"Nothing," Kerry muttered.

"Come on, don't play games. I'm your best friend, *remember?*"

Kerry managed a weak smile. She was so happy in her temporary home, despite Whitney and their never-ending feuding. She wished she never had to leave. Then she thought about her father and began to wonder if what she planned to do with the five hundred dollars was a good idea. Not that she'd even gotten the precious money yet, but she was determined to try her best. And she hadn't even told Holly about her plans. Yet. Maybe *now* was the time to share her secret.

She cleared her throat nervously. "Holly," she said slowly, "*if* I get to ride in the movie, I'm going to buy myself a horse with the five hundred dollars." From the look on Holly's face, Kerry could tell she'd really surprised her.

"A horse? For five hundred dollars?" Holly was astonished. "You've got to be kidding."

"Uh-uh," Kerry shot back at her friend, her green eyes flashing with defiance. "Look at this list!" She waved her hand toward the notice board. "Do you see anything wrong with it? Like that *blank* space beside my name?"

"But, Kerry, you don't even know how long you're staying at Timber Ridge, and what will your father say?"

"He won't mind." Kerry crossed her fingers, hoping it wasn't a whopping lie.

"But a horse for five hundred dollars," Holly persisted. "Wow, you might just be able to afford the ears and the tail for that. But nothing in between!"

"Horses don't have to be expensive," Kerry argued.

"Good ones are. Susan's horse cost five thousand, not five hundred dollars."

Kerry avoided looking Holly straight in the eye, knowing she wasn't kidding. Tara, Susan's new dapple gray mare, wasn't even considered a top-quality horse either. She was a good, steady jumper and did okay in the dressage ring. But she wasn't nearly as good as Buccaneer or even Magician.

"Have you told Mom yet?" Holly asked gently.

Kerry shook her head. "You're the only one who knows, and please don't tell anyone. If Whitney found out, it'd only make her even more determined to beat me and get the part."

"Who else do you think will try out?"

"Robin, maybe Jennifer," Kerry replied quietly.

"And you, and Whitney," Holly finished for her. "I wonder if Sue will try out as well."

Kerry hoped not. The more kids involved, the less her chance of winning. "Holly, promise you won't tell Liz, okay? Not till I win. Then I'll ask her to help me find a horse."

"Boy, you're confident, aren't you?" Holly teased good-naturedly.

"Not really, but it helps to pretend I am."

"You know this will only stir up the old trouble again, don't you?" Holly said grimly.

"Whitney?"

"You bet. She's probably at home right now, plotting and planning her revenge already. You'd better watch out. I don't think she's finished with you yet."

Kerry nodded glumly. Ever since she'd arrived at Timber Ridge, Whitney Myers had done everything she could to force her into leaving. It had been one rotten trick after another, and because of Whitney's jealousy, Kerry had almost lost her job.

On her way back to the house, Kerry tried to figure out what made Whitney so impossible. The only reason she could come up with was Whitney's mother. Mrs. Myers was always pushing her daughter to win blue ribbons; and with Kerry on the riding team, Whitney wasn't doing as well as she used to. Kerry was a far better rider, and Whitney was insanely jealous of that.

Then she started to worry about the screen test. She wondered what Whitney could do to make her look like a fool.

She knew she wouldn't have to wait long to find out. Mr. Ballantine had promised to phone Liz within the next couple of days to set up the shooting schedule. With any luck, the whole thing would be over within no time, and with even more luck, she could start looking for the perfect horse.

Chapter Two

Kerry swam lazily around the Chapmans' swimming pool, every now and then glancing up toward Timber Ridge Mountain. It towered over everything, dwarfing the trees and houses that clustered around its base. The ski trails were still fresh and green with midsummer grass. Kerry idly wondered what it would look like in winter. She'd never skied before and really wanted to try.

Suddenly the phone rang, pushing all thoughts of the mountain out of her mind. Maybe it was Giles Ballantine with news of the screen test. Kerry swam to the edge of the pool and climbed out just as Holly came out of the kitchen door.

"Mr. Ballantine said he wants you to be ready to ride in a preliminary screen test tomorrow morning!" Holly yelled.

Kerry's heart jumped with nerves and excitement. This was it! The moment she'd been waiting for. She picked up her towel and ran toward the house. "Where's Liz? I need to talk to her."

"In her office."

Kerry ran down the hallway and skidded around the corner into the spare bedroom that Liz used as an office. "Hey, Liz, what will I have to do in the screen test?" she asked nervously. Liz was sitting at her desk, grumpily doing the one thing she hated most. Paperwork!

"Just ride," Liz said shortly as she shuffled through a pile of papers, looking for something. "Ah, there it is." She snatched up the stable's green ledger book.

"But what *kind* of riding?" Kerry insisted, feeling her nerves jangling around inside her. "Will I have to jump, or fall off—or what?"

Liz smiled and put the book down. "You sound like a kid off to her first horse show," she said in a gentle voice. "Stop worrying about it, Kerry. So what if you don't get the part. It won't be the end of the world."

The end of *my* world, Kerry thought to herself dramatically. "Come on, Liz, surely Mr. Ballantine said *something*."

"All he wants you to do is be ready to ride with the other girls at nine o'clock. He wants to see all of you in the ring at once, and then he's going to choose two of you to take the screen test. That's all."

Kerry's stomach heaved, her mouth went dry, and her hands got sweaty. "What should I wear?"

Liz burst out laughing. "You're not supposed to say things like that till you're older and going out on dates," she teased. "Just wear a pair of breeches, and don't forget your hard hat. And," she added

17

gently, "you'll do fine, so stop feeling so insecure."

Holly burst into the office clutching a brown envelope. "Guess what just arrived," she shrieked as she tore it open.

"What?"

"The story outline for the scene. Mr. Ballantine's assistant just dropped it off." She grabbed Kerry's hand and pulled her into the family room.

Kerry threw herself onto the couch and waited impatiently for Holly to finish reading the first page.

"Wow!" Holly cried breathlessly as she handed Kerry the first page of the outline. "You gotta read this. If you get the part, you're going to have quite a ride!"

Kerry read quickly. The scene in which she *hoped* to ride had the film's young star being chased through the fields and woods by a bunch of villains on motorcycles. The girl was on horseback and had to ride at a full gallop across a field, go into the woods, and take several jumps in her efforts to get away from her would-be attackers. But since they were on hopped-up motorcycles, they were able to jump them over the obstacles and keep on following her.

"How does it end?" Kerry asked. Holly was still reading the second page, her eyes opening wider and wider.

"Doesn't really say," she said when she'd finished reading. "It ends with the girl on the horse riding over the last jump, and looking around her as the guys following her start to catch up." She grinned. "They always leave you in suspense like this in movies, don't they?"

Kerry nodded. "Yeah, and the next scene shows the heroine is perfectly okay and ready for the next disaster!" Kerry began to wonder if Whitney was also reading the story outline.

Holly was obviously thinking the same thing, because she started to chuckle. "I'd give anything to see Whitney being chased through the woods by a bunch of guys in leather jackets, riding motor-cycles."

"Maybe she'll drop out," Kerry suggested hopefully.

"Fat chance," Holly retorted. "But she'll probably get her mother to tie her in the saddle before she tries anything this hairy!"

Kerry was in the barn by six-thirty the next morning. She wanted to groom Magician to perfection so that Giles Ballantine couldn't refuse to choose him—*and* her—for the screen test.

One by one, the other girls arrived. By nine o'clock all five of them were mounted on their horses, eagerly waiting for the riding test to start.

Mrs. Myers arrived with Mr. Ballantine. She ran up to her daughter and patted her knee reassuringly. Whitney flashed a confident smile, as if she knew this was only a formality. In her mind Giles Ballantine was sure to choose her. After the gourmet meal her mother had served him the previous night, he would have no other choice.

"Okay, girls," Mr. Ballantine's voice boomed out. "Just go into the ring, spread out, and walk around for a few minutes. I want to get a real good look at all of your horses."

Kerry felt his admiring eyes on Magician as she trotted past him, and she was glad she'd spent the extra hour grooming her horse. She hoped Mr. Ballantine preferred black horses. The other four were one gray, one dark bay, and two chestnuts. Maybe black horses photographed really well. She hoped they did.

It was almost like being in a horse show, Kerry thought as she trotted and cantered around the ring in front of the critical movie producer. Liz had joined him in the middle of the ring, and she smiled at Kerry as the girl cantered past her.

Then Mr. Ballantine called them all into the center of the ring and told them to line up. This was really getting more and more like a horse show, but much more was at stake than a blue ribbon—at least for Kerry!

Mr. Ballantine then whispered a few words into Liz's ear, and she walked off toward one of the jumps. While she was adjusting it, the movie producer walked carefully around each horse and made notes on the clipboard he was carrying. Kerry was dying with curiosity and impatience, but she fought hard to control it. She sat perfectly still, her eyes forward, and prayed Magician wouldn't start fidgeting.

"I want each of you to jump the three fences over there," he said when he'd finally finished his close examination. "Whitney, you go first, my dear."

Whitney smiled at him sweetly, gathered up her reins, and let her well-trained horse take her effortlessly over the jumps. They weren't very high, and she did it perfectly. She knew it, too. Her face wore

a triumphant smile when she returned to the group.

One by one, the other three riders had their turn, and each one of them performed very well. Kerry went last, and her nerves were really on edge. "Don't let me down!" she whispered urgently to her horse as they approached the first jump.

Magician flicked his ears and flew over the brush jump, the double oxer, and the five-bar gate as if they were nothing more than tiny shoe boxes. Kerry heaved a sigh of relief as they cleared the last fence. It was all over, and she knew they'd done well, too.

"Okay, kids, that's enough," Mr. Ballantine said in a hearty voice. "Just cool your horses off, and if you want, you can put them back in their stalls. I just want to have a word with Liz, then I'll tell you who the lucky two are."

It was the longest ten minutes of Kerry's life.

She couldn't sit still, so she ended up pacing up and down the aisle, eating all of Buccaneer's M&M's. Finally, when Kerry thought she couldn't stand it any longer, Liz stuck her head in the barn and told the girls to come out.

They all clustered around the movie producer, nervous and excited.

"First of all," Mr. Ballantine said with a smile, "thanks for trying out. All of you are terrific riders, and if that was all I had to base my decision on, it'd be a real hard choice. But"—he paused dramatically and looked at them closely—"I had to consider your horses as well. The horse in this scene has got to be spirited and show excitement." He turned to Susan first. "Your little gray mare is very pretty, but she's too quiet. I'm afraid I won't be able to use you. I'm sorry."

One down, two to go, Kerry thought. But which two? She could feel her heart thumping loudly inside her and hoped no one else could. Faintly she heard Mr. Ballantine talking to Jennifer. He was saying something about her horse being too small. Kerry glanced at her friend. Jennifer looked disappointed, but she was doing her best to smile anyway.

Then he turned to face Kerry, and her heart almost stopped beating. This is it, she thought miserably as an enormous wave of disappointment flooded over her. But the producer's eyes kept moving and settled on Robin, who was standing next to her.

"Same problem as the gray mare," he said kindly. "Not enough spirit. But thanks anyway."

Kerry let out a huge sigh of relief as Holly started jumping up and down excitedly. "You got it!" she squealed at the top of her voice.

"Not yet," Whitney's sneering voice said clearly behind them. "She's got to beat *me* in the screen test first."

Kerry's elation evaporated as if someone had dumped a bucket of cold water over her. Whitney was right. This was only the first round in the contest, and a much more difficult one faced both of them.

Giles Ballantine put his arm around Kerry's shoulders. "Okay, girls. I want you two to be ready to ride your screen test for me tomorrow morning. I'll have the film crew here early, and we're going to use the meadow by the cross-country course."

"Will we have to ride the scene just like in the story

23

outline?" Kerry asked quietly. The vivid description of the hair-raising ride didn't bother her anymore, but she was still curious how Whitney felt about it.

"Just a bit of it," Giles answered. "Enough so I can see what you'll be like over bigger jumps with the woods around you. We're setting up the cameras this afternoon, and all you two have to do is pray it doesn't rain."

Kerry glanced up at the cloudless blue sky and crossed her fingers. She didn't think she could stand to wait even the necessary twenty-four hours, let alone endure a delay because of bad weather.

Robin, Sue, and Jennifer crowded around her when she got back inside the barn.

"Bet you're excited," Jennifer said with a touch of envy in her voice. "I wish I'd been picked."

"Lucky you," Robin said, echoing Jennifer's emotions.

Sue didn't say anything. She just smiled happily at Kerry and patted her on the back.

"I'm scared to death," Kerry admitted to her as she leaned against Tara's stall door and watched Sue brushing her new horse. She felt a brief pang of envy. If everything went according to plan and she won the part in the film, *she* would be brushing her own horse pretty soon.

That evening Kerry suddenly realized she had no idea what she ought to wear for the actual screen test.

"Not again," Liz groaned when Kerry asked her opinion. "I thought we'd settled that yesterday."

"But, Liz," Kerry protested, "that was only for riding around in the ring. This is the real thing. Suppose I turn up wearing something really stupid."

Liz grinned. "You don't exactly have a large choice, do you?" she said in a teasing tone. "Or were you planning on a long dress and a fur cape?"

"Don't tease me, Liz," Kerry implored. "You know what I mean. Should I wear riding breeches and my black boots, or do you think I ought to wear jeans? Help me, *please*!"

"Look, if you're so hung up on your wardrobe, why don't you just phone the Myers and ask Giles yourself? He's staying with them till the screen test is over."

Kerry shook her head. "With my luck, Whitney will answer the phone. You do it. Please."

"Okay." Liz reached for the phone on her desk and dialed the Myerses' number. Kerry went to join Holly in the family room.

"All right," Liz said a few minutes later. "Here's the story. Giles and Mr. and Mrs. Myers have gone out to dinner, but Whitney says she's wearing jeans and a work shirt. So there's your answer."

"Hah," Holly retorted. "When was the last time anyone saw Whitney in jeans and a work shirt?"

Liz shrugged, then disappeared back inside her office.

"Now what?" Kerry muttered.

"Simple," Holly said brightly. "You know Whitney's lying. She wants you to turn up looking like a jerk. You can bet your life she'll be dressed to kill, so why don't you call her bluff?"

"You're right," Kerry declared in a firm voice. "I'll wear my best white breeches, and I'll go and polish my boots right now. Hey, maybe I ought to wear my black hunt jacket as well."

"Don't overdo it," Holly said with a laugh. "I'll lend you my new dress shirt."

"Thanks," Kerry said gratefully. She knew how much Holly treasured that shirt, but it was just perfect.

Got you, Whitney Myers, Kerry thought happily as she smeared the sticky black shoe polish onto her riding boots. You're expecting me to turn up looking like a cowboy, but I'm smarter than you think!

Chapter Three

"Wow! Just look at all those people!" Holly exclaimed in amazement as she and Kerry rode toward the meadow at the start of the cross-country course. They had switched horses, and Kerry was riding Buccaneer so that Holly could ride the more reliable Magician on the half-mile trail through the woods from the barn.

Kerry pulled off her hard hat and ran her hand through her thick, brown hair. Although it was still early enough to be cool, her head felt hot and sweaty. Cramming the hat back on, she stared at the large, open field. Overnight, it had been transformed into a jungle. There were people, arc lamps, wires and cables, a loudspeaker system, and an enormous white tent in front of them.

"Where did all *this* come from?" Kerry asked in astonishment. Buccaneer's ears were pricked forward, and already he was prancing nervously as he saw the strange sights around him. Kerry glanced over at Holly and Magician. Her friend's horse was taking it all much more calmly, and Kerry was glad she'd chosen him to ride in her screen test.

A young man with wild, frizzy, red hair and sunglasses ran up to them waving a clipboard. He glanced briefly at Kerry, then turned toward Holly. "Are you the one riding the screen test?"

Holly shook her head. "No, but this *is* the right horse," and she carefully got off Magician's back. The young man introduced himself as Tony Gibson, Giles Ballantine's first assistant director.

Kerry blushed as Tony's eyes swept over her critically. Then he frowned, and she wondered what was wrong.

"Is that the outfit you're going to wear?" he asked.

Kerry wished she could see his eyes. But as she studied his face, all she could see was her own slightly distorted reflection in the young man's mirrored sunglasses. "It's okay, isn't it?" she asked anxiously, glancing down at her white breeches.

"I guess so," Tony said, and then he shrugged his shoulders. "I don't know anything about horses or riding outfits, but didn't the other girl tell you what to wear?" Suddenly someone yelled his name, and he wandered off and in seconds was lost in the crowd of people and equipment.

Kerry's confidence started to waver. She looked around wildly for a glimpse of Whitney or Astronaut, but there were too many people in the way. She told herself angrily that she should have ignored Holly's protests and gone ahead and worn her black hunt jacket. Whitney was probably all decked out in a classical dressage outfit with a long-tailed riding coat and a top hat.

She kicked her stirrups free and jumped off Buccaneer's back. Then she traded horses with Holly and helped her friend back into the saddle. This time on Buccaneer. "Be good," she warned the horse sternly. "If you let her fall off, I'll never give you any more M and M's!"

"I wonder where Whitney is," Holly said as her eyes scanned the masses of people and strange equipment that was all crowded into one corner of the enormous meadow. "And where's Mr. Ballantine?"

"There he is, over there!" Kerry cried. She'd just vaulted into Magician's saddle and had spotted the movie producer by a large blue camper van. He was talking to Liz, who had just arrived.

"Still no sign of Whitney, huh?" Holly muttered. "She's got to be here someplace. Tony said he'd seen her."

Just then, Buccaneer picked up his head from the grass he'd been munching on and neighed loudly.

"There she is," Kerry said as the girl on horseback emerged from the woods that bordered the meadow. "I bet she's been practicing over the jumps."

"Don't sweat it," Holly said casually. "She needs the practice. You don't."

Kerry wasn't listening to her. Her mouth fell open, and as Whitney and Astronaut rode toward them, she realized that Whitney had won the first round.

"She tricked us," Holly said angrily, staring at Whitney's riding outfit.

29

"No, I didn't." Whitney heard her and trotted up on a slightly sweaty Astronaut. "I *told* you I was wearing jeans and a work shirt." Then she stared contemptuously at Kerry and laughed. "Boy, do you look dumb, Kerry Logan. You ought to be in a wedding in that outfit. It's all *white*!"

Kerry blushed bright red. Giles Ballantine had arrived just in time to hear Whitney's sarcastic remark. She wanted to die with embarrassment, but she was stuck. There was nothing she could do. Unless . . . She glanced at Holly's jeans and blue and white checked shirt.

Ignoring everyone else, Kerry whispered urgently to her friend. "Come on, we've got to change clothes. I can't ride in this."

Mr. Ballantine confirmed her decision. "Hmmm, I really wanted you to look more casual than this," he said, eyeing Kerry's spotless white breeches and shirt. Then he waved toward Whitney, who was looking very smug. "More like what *she's* wearing."

Whitney laughed, her eyes flashing with triumph. "Too bad," she sneered at Kerry under her breath.

"I'll only take a second to change," Kerry muttered apologetically. "Can we use your van?"

Mr. Ballantine smiled. "Sure, and don't hurry. Whitney's going to ride first, so you've got plenty of time."

"Trust Whitney to make me look like a fool," Kerry grumbled to Holly as they walked their horses toward Giles Ballantine's camper van.

"It was *my* fault," Holly said with an embarrassed

laugh. "I'm the one who told you to do the opposite."

"That's okay." Kerry was just thankful that she and Holly were more or less the same size. Now all she had to do was change clothes with her and try to put her shattered nerves back together again.

Liz held both their horses for them while they switched clothes inside the van.

"Much better," Tony, the assistant director, said when Kerry came out wearing Holly's faded jeans and checked shirt. She'd kept her own riding boots on, but had pulled the jeans down over them so only her foot showed below the cuff.

"Come on," Holly said as they took their horses from Liz. "Let's go over by the hedge and keep out of the way. We ought to be able to see Whitney make a fool of herself from there."

"What makes you so sure she's going to mess up?" Kerry asked as she jumped down off Magician's back and flopped to the ground. The horse immediately put his nose down and started eating the lush grass and weeds that were growing around his feet.

"Just a hunch."

"I wish *I* were riding first," Kerry muttered enviously, watching Whitney as she sat on her horse, listening to Giles Ballantine's instructions.

"Don't be stupid," Holly retorted. "This is perfect. This way you get to see any mistakes she makes, and you'll have a much better chance of doing it right. Come on, Kerry. You know she'll mess it up."

Kerry wasn't sure she agreed. The way her stomach was turning somersaults, all she wanted was to have it over and done with. "Holly, I'm really scared," she blurted out. "I don't trust Whitney. I just know she's going to pull something on me."

"Out here? You're crazy! There must be over fifty people in this field. What on earth could she do to foul things up with everyone watching?"

Kerry gritted her teeth and tried not to think about all the other times Whitney had tried to cause her trouble. Instead she tried hard to relax. But the nagging feeling that Whitney would do almost anything to get the part in the film wouldn't go away.

After Whitney and Astronaut had ridden the practice course in the meadow several times, Giles Ballantine took the film crew into the woods. Kerry and Holly decided to remain where they were. They were out of everyone's way, sitting by the hedge.

Kerry's tension mounted while they were gone, and to keep herself from going crazy, she absentmindedly started to play with a stalk of prickly thistles. They were growing everywhere by the hedge, and already several of their tiny, sharp burrs had firmly attached themselves to her pants legs. She pulled them off, wincing as their sharp little prickers pierced her fingers.

"I'm thirsty," Holly said. She got up stiffly and looped Buccaneer's reins over her arm. "I'm going to get a soda. Do you want one?"

Kerry shook her head. Whitney and Astronaut had just emerged from the woods with the mobile film crew, and she felt too nervous to drink anything. "I'll wait here," she said as Holly started to lead Buccaneer toward the tent.

Whitney detached herself from the group and

cantered up to Kerry and Magician. "Mr. Ballantine wants to talk to you," she said with a triumphant look. It was obvious that the filming in the woods had gone well. Kerry pulled Magician's head up from the grass and tightened his girth.

"Don't waste time," Whitney snapped impatiently. "Just run over there yourself. I'll hold Magician for you." Whitney dismounted quickly and grabbed the horse's reins from Kerry's hands before she had a chance to argue. "Go on," she said sharply. "Don't keep him waiting."

"Ah, there you are," Mr. Ballantine said when Kerry ran up to him, slightly out of breath. She glanced back over her shoulder. Whitney was still standing by the hedge, holding Astronaut and Magician.

"You saw what Whitney did, didn't you?" the movie producer continued.

Kerry nodded.

"I want you to do exactly the same kind of thing. We'll start off in this field. You can warm up over the practice fences, and after a couple of gallops, we'll go into the woods."

Whitney walked up with Astronaut and Magician. She gave a fake smile as she handed Kerry her horse's reins. "What a stupid waste of time," she muttered under her breath as Kerry took her horse away from her. "But I guess he feels sorry for you, Kerry." She hesitated, and then added in a sickly sweet voice, "Good luck, but it won't do you any good. I've won the part, and we both know it."

Kerry glared at her, deciding not to answer. She couldn't trust herself not to be rude, and with Giles

Ballantine and Liz standing within earshot, she didn't want to make a scene.

"Okay, boy," Kerry whispered nervously to Magician as she tightened his girth. The horse unexpectedly laid his ears back and tried to nip at her arm. For a second Kerry hesitated before putting her foot in the stirrup.

That was odd! Magician never minded having his girth tightened. Some horses did, but not him.

Maybe he's as nervous as I am, Kerry thought to herself as she swung her leg over his back and settled herself in the saddle.

That was the last sensible thought she had. As soon as Magician felt her weight on his back, he went crazy. With an angry squeal, the big, black horse erupted in a frenzy and reared up in the air, his forelegs flailing wildly in front of him.

As she hung on to his back for dear life, Kerry saw her precious screen test disappear in a puff of smoke before her panic-stricken eyes.

Chapter Four

"Kerry, hold on tight!"

"Someone—stop him!"

"He's gone crazy."

Kerry could barely hear them. As Magician bucked and plunged with explosive energy, all that she was aware of was a blur of faces through his whiplike mane, and people scrambling to get out of her way.

Kerry felt like a tiny ship being tossed around on a gigantic wave as Magician's bucks grew stronger. She frantically curled her fingers through his mane and gripped as hard as she could with her legs in her efforts to stay on his gyrating back.

Just when she thought she was going to be thrown off him, Liz's voice penetrated her confused mind. "Hit him between the ears. Use your crop!"

Crop? Did she have one? As the horse leaped into yet another violent buck, her head snapped forward, and she saw her crop. Still in her right hand,

along with a chunk of mane. She tore her hand loose and, with a mighty swing of her right arm, brought the crop down hard between Magician's ears. She felt a brief moment of guilt at hitting him, but then it was gone. She knew it was the only thing that could save her.

All of a sudden Magician's violent movements stopped. As soon as his forelegs hit the ground, Kerry threw herself clear and landed with a thud, narrowly missing his hooves. Magician let off one more buck, and then stopped. He was trembling all over.

For a second Kerry was dazed and didn't know where she was. Then a pair of strong arms wrapped themselves around her, and she felt herself being lifted to her feet.

"Magician?" she croaked out. "Is he okay?"

"He's fine," Giles Ballantine said gently. "But what about you?" He held her firmly, and she leaned against him, grateful for his support. Her legs felt like jelly, and she was shaking horribly.

Liz came up, leading the frightened horse. As she peered anxiously at Kerry's bleached-out face, she patted the horse's neck and spoke soothingly to him. "I don't understand," she said in a worried voice to both Kerry and Giles. "He's *never* acted like this before. Something must be terribly wrong."

"Well, I guess that's that, then," Giles Ballantine said. He sounded disappointed.

"What do you mean?" Kerry blurted out. His words sounded so final. In a panic, she realized that he was telling her that her chance to ride in the screen test was over. She, or rather her horse, had just blown it.

"Wait a minute . . ." Kerry muttered, breaking loose from his arm. Something she'd read once, about a normally well-behaved horse going suddenly out of control, had just flashed through her mind, and it just might solve the mystery of Magician's crazy behavior.

Kerry quietly approached the horse. He'd stopped trembling, but the whites of his eyes were showing, and he had flecks of sweat on his neck. Gently Kerry pressed down on his saddle. Magician immediately squealed and lashed out with his hind feet.

Holly handed Buccaneer's reins to Mr. Ballantine and limped up to Kerry. "Are you okay?" she whispered anxiously. "You scared me to death. I thought for sure Magician was going to kill you!"

"I'm fine," Kerry said. Then she carefully released the buckles on Magician's saddle and let his girth drop to the ground. "I *knew* it!" she exclaimed as she lifted up the saddle.

"What is it?" Liz was still standing by the horse's head, stroking his face, and holding his bridle firmly with her other hand.

"Prickers!" Holly gasped, staring at the three squashed up burrs in the palm of Kerry's hand.

"You got it. But what I want to know is, how did they get there?"

"Holly, come and hold him for me," Liz said sharply. While Holly took over the job of standing at Magician's head, Liz joined Kerry and looked at the tiny pieces of torture that had almost driven the horse crazy.

Kerry shook her head. "I know I didn't take his

saddle off while I was waiting. There's no way one of these things could've gotten under there by themselves."

"Okay, folks," Giles's loud voice boomed out. "That's a wrap. Let's start packing up."

Kerry caught a glimpse of Whitney's sneering face when she looked up from the evidence in her hand. Of course! It couldn't be anything—or anyone— else. No wonder Whitney was so "helpful" a few minutes ago by offering to hold on to Magician while she ran over to talk to Mr. Ballantine. It wouldn't have taken her but a few seconds to ram a bunch of prickers under the poor animal's saddle.

A cold fury seeped through Kerry, and she had to fight hard to choke down the angry, accusing words that were already forming on her lips. "No, wait!" she yelled out to the movie producer who was already heading back toward his van. "I still want to ride the screen test."

"Kerry," Liz said quickly, "you can't ride him. Look what those burrs did to his skin. It's all raw. He'll go nuts if you try and put that saddle back on him."

Kerry groaned. She hadn't noticed the tiny spot where the vicious prickers had already rubbed away Magician's hair, leaving spots of blood oozing out of his withers. In desperation she thought about riding Buccaneer, but she knew he was much too nervous. It had to be Magician and it had to be now!

"Did I hear you say you were going to ride the screen test after all?" Giles Ballantine said. He put his arm roughly around Kerry's shoulders again. "That's the spirit, young lady." Then he turned to his

40

assistant director. "Cancel my last order, Tony. Kerry's going to ride."

"But she can't ride," Liz protested violently. "That poor horse can't stand a saddle on his back. Not with that ugly sore he's got."

"I'm going to ride him bareback," Kerry said quietly.

Liz wasn't the only one who was surprised. Whitney had rejoined the group, and right now she was staring angrily at Kerry with an incredulous expression on her face. "But you *can't*," she sputtered. "You'll never get over those jumps in the woods without a saddle."

"I've been jumping bareback since I was five," Kerry snapped. It was a slight exaggeration, but she didn't care. If Whitney was allowed to lie and cheat, so could she.

"Kerry, do you really think you can do it?" Holly's face lit up in a hopeful smile.

Kerry nodded. "Yup, and as long as it doesn't bother Magician, I'm going to try." She turned toward Liz. "Will you give me a leg up?"

Liz started to protest, and then she saw the determined look on Kerry's face. "I think you're out of your mind," she said as she bent down and hoisted Kerry over the horse's back, "but I know how much this means to you. Just don't try anything you know you can't handle, okay?"

Magician trembled when he felt the weight on his back, but he didn't put his ears back, or try to kick out. Kerry gathered up the reins and looked down at the tiny sore patch again. Luckily, her thighs

41

weren't going to touch it.

"Good luck!" Holly yelled as Kerry walked Magician toward Giles Ballantine and the camera crew.

Before Kerry had the chance to ask him what he wanted her to do first, Whitney pushed in front of her and grabbed at Magician's bridle. "She can't ride this scene bareback, Mr. Ballantine. It's much too dangerous. It's totally irresponsible. A good rider would never do such a thing. *I* certainly wouldn't try it!" Then she whirled around and glared angrily at Kerry. "You're a fool," she spat out. "You'll never get over the Hog's Back. They've built it straight up."

Kerry ignored Whitney's warning. She knew the girl was only trying to scare her off so *she'd* get the part by default. "Let go of my bridle!" she said coldly. "You're in my way."

For a moment Whitney hesitated. Then her arm fell to her side. "It's *your* funeral," she spat out venomously.

"Are you sure you can handle this?" Mr. Ballantine asked her gently as Whitney stalked off with her head in the air.

"Yes."

"I don't want you taking any chances now. If you can't handle it, then I'll just give the part to Whitney."

Over my dead body, Kerry thought to herself angrily, but she forced herself to smile as Mr. Ballantine told her again what he wanted her to do. When he'd finished, he barked out a string of orders to his crew and then told Kerry to wait for his signal.

42

She trotted Magician over to the beginning of the practice course. She'd never ridden him bareback before, but luckily he was fairly comfortable. He didn't have sharp, knifelike withers. As she urged him into a slow canter, she felt her confidence returning. It wasn't going to be as easy as it would have been *with* her saddle, but she wasn't going to give up. She still had a chance, and she was determined to make the best of it, in spite of Whitney's desperate efforts to ruin everything.

As she cantered her horse over the small practice jumps, she promised Magician she would feed him ten pounds of fresh carrots that night. His ears were pricked forward, and his stride was even and steady. He paced himself perfectly between the jumps, and all she had to do was sit there and guide him along the course.

Giles Ballantine's voice boomed out at her just as she was about to jump the course for a third time. "That's enough!" he shouted through his bullhorn. "That was terrific. Now, just turn him up the field and gallop as fast as you can."

Magician needed no urging. It was as if he'd understood the producer's orders, because in a flash he was off, streaking up the slight hill toward the far hedge. Kerry hunched herself over his shoulders and grasped his flying mane. They raced to the end of the field, turned around, and cantered back to the group by the tent.

Holly's grim expression, when she finally reached her, told her that her friend had figured out how the prickers had gotten under Magician's saddle.

"Don't say anything," Kerry warned urgently.

"Why not? *She* did it," Holly snapped. "I'm going to tell Mom."

"Don't. Just let it go. We can't prove it, and you know she'll deny everything, just like always."

"But Mom'll believe us," Holly protested.

"It doesn't matter. I don't want to worry about what she'll do to Whitney while I'm riding the cross country. She can't get me out there as long as she stays here."

"I'll make sure she does," Holly replied grimly. "Don't worry. I'll tie her up if I have to."

Kerry grinned and started to feel better.

"How did it feel?" Liz strode up to her, a smile on her face.

"Great. I'd have ridden him bareback before if I'd known how comfortable he was."

"Well, just don't take any chances on that cross-country course," Liz muttered. "There's a big difference between those fences and these little ones out here."

As soon as Giles Ballantine had organized his camera crew, Kerry trotted after him toward the start of the cross-country course. The first jump had a platform to one side, with a large camera mounted on top. Magician snorted when he saw the strange equipment, so Kerry quietly urged him toward it, letting the animal check it out for himself. Satisfied that it wasn't going to hurt him, Magician relaxed and put his ears forward.

45

"Okay!" she cried out. "We're ready!"

Magician jumped the first fence with only a sideways glance at the camera beside it. And by the time they reached the next jump, his stride didn't even falter as they soared over the top of it.

"Hog's Back comes next," Kerry said to herself as she crouched into Magician's flying mane. As the steep jump came into view, she tensed slightly. Whitney had been right. It did go straight up—and worst of all it was absolutely impossible to see what was on the other side. She twined her fingers tightly through the horse's mane as he took off. They landed safely on the other side, and Kerry heaved a sigh of relief as they galloped toward the stream.

"Don't even *think* about swimming!" Kerry threatened her horse as he splashed noisily into the cool water. Magician loved water, and unless she kept him moving he'd lie down and roll in it. She urged him forward through the shallow water and glanced toward the camera that was focused on her and Magician. She began to feel like a real movie star and flashed a smile in its direction.

"Good work!" Giles Ballantine yelled out encouragingly. "Keep it up."

Kerry grinned even wider and leaned forward on her horse as he lurched up the steep bank on the other side of the stream. There were only two more fences, and things were going just great. Magician roared up and over the log jump with his rider crouched low on his neck, her hands still entwined around his mane.

Just as her confidence reached new heights, disaster struck! Magician's hind foot slipped out from underneath him as he took off over the last jump, and the last thing Kerry remembered was flying over his head, wondering if the camera was catching it all.

Then she hit the ground, and everything went black.

Chapter Five

"Kerry, are you okay? Say something!" The gruff, but kindly voice paused. "No, you idiot, don't move her. She may have broken something."

Giles Ballantine's words jolted the fuzziness out of Kerry's bewildered mind. "I'm fine," she protested as she struggled to sit up. Then she grimaced as a jolt of pain seared through her shoulder. "What happened?" she finally croaked out in a hoarse whisper. "Is Magician hurt? Where is he?" She looked around wildly, then relaxed when she saw her horse standing quietly beside Tony Gibson.

"He's fine," Mr. Ballantine assured her in a soothing voice. "It's you I'm worried about."

"Just a few bruises," Kerry muttered, and hoped she was right. Her shoulder felt as if someone were sticking hot needles into it, and as Giles Ballantine helped her to her feet, she prayed she hadn't done any serious damage.

"Your horse slipped on a patch of wet leaves," he said as he steadied the trembling young rider. Kerry was still very shaky and her face was deathly white. "He got over the jump okay, but I'm afraid you didn't. You landed right on top of it." Then he paused. "Are you *sure* you're all right? I think we ought to have that shoulder of yours x-rayed."

"It's fine," Kerry lied, and pulled her hand away from her arm where she'd been helping to support her injured shoulder. She didn't have time to worry about a few bruises—if that's all that was wrong. "Will I . . . have I lost . . . ?" she stuttered, trying to ask the question that was burning a hole in her mind.

Giles Ballantine laughed. "Boy, you're one determined kid, I'll say that for you. And no, you haven't lost your chance for the part."

"Then you mean . . ." She was too embarrassed to finish.

He laughed again. "Hold on, young lady. I didn't say you'd *gotten* it. I just meant you're still in the running."

Kerry's hopes for an immediate decision were dashed as he continued.

"I've got to get all the film we shot today off to the lab for processing, and then I have to look at it closely before I make my decision." He paused and smiled kindly. "You and Whitney both rode very well, and my decision won't be based on who's the best rider. It's more a matter of who photographs the best."

"Oh." She'd hoped he would announce the winner right away, but of course he had to see the film first. How could she have been so dumb? That was the whole point of the screen test.

When she got back to the meadow, news of her fall had already reached Holly and Liz.

"Hey, you don't suppose they got your wipeout on film, do you?" Holly asked with a grin while her mother anxiously examined Kerry's injured shoulder.

"I guess they did," Kerry said with a wince as Liz gently pressed her upper arm.

"Wouldn't it be great if Giles Ballantine decided to use it in the real film. I mean, then he'd *have* to use you for the part instead of Whitney."

Kerry giggled at her friend's hopeful expression. "Nah, that wouldn't work. If the girl in the scene fell off, then the motorcycle crowd would be able to catch her. The scene doesn't end that way, remember?"

"He could always rewrite it."

Kerry told her to stop fantasizing, and that Giles Ballantine had to look at his film before he decided between her and Whitney.

"But he's *got* to choose you," Holly said defiantly. "You're much better than Whitney, and besides," she added with a scowl, "none of us will be able to live with her if she gets the part."

"We won't be able to live with her if she *doesn't*."

"Yeah, we lose either way, huh?" Holly said. They both broke up with laughter.

Liz insisted on taking Kerry to the clinic for test, and when the radiologist told them that nothing was broken, Kerry heaved a sigh of relief. Her shoulder still hurt like mad, but as long as Giles Ballantine didn't schedule the shooting for at least another week, she knew she'd be okay. Now all she had to do was wait and hope for the best.

She got her answer the next day. Giles Ballantine phoned and told Kerry to meet him at the barn.

Holly and Kerry were already waiting when Mr. Ballantine's dark red Mercedes pulled into the driveway. Whitney was with him, and for a horrible moment Kerry imagined she could see signs of triumph on the girl's sneering face as they all went into Liz's office. Maybe Mr. Ballantine had already told Whitney *she* was getting the part. Kerry's nerves settled into a tight knot in the pit of her stomach. She could imagine his first words . . . "I'm terribly sorry, Kerry, but Whitney . . ."

Giles Ballantine settled himself in the chair in front of Liz's desk. "Okay, girls, here's the story," he said with a smile. "You both rode fantastically well, and the horses were very photogenic . . ."

Here it comes, Kerry thought gloomily as a surge of disappointment washed over her. She held her breath and closed her eyes. Visions of Whitney preening in front of a camera floated in front of her.

"It wasn't an easy decision," Giles Ballantine continued, "and I had to run the film many times before I made up my mind."

"Please tell us!" Holly blurted out.

"Shhh," Kerry hissed at her.

Mr. Ballantine turned and smiled at Whitney. Her expression changed from contented sneer to glorious triumph. "Whitney," he said gently, "you were spectacular out there, and your Astronaut is a fine-looking horse, but . . ."

Whitney suddenly stopped smiling.

"But . . ." the movie producer continued in a smooth voice, "I've decided to use Kerry for the part."

"Whoopee!" Holly cried out, and almost fell off the end of the tack trunk.

Kerry was too stunned to say anything.

Whitney's face turned bright red. She glared at Kerry. "But *why?* I'm a much better rider than she is!" she choked out, her words clipped and angry.

"Because she rode the scene bareback," Giles Ballantine explained patiently. "And when I saw the film of her, I decided it was absolutely perfect. And I remembered, Whitney, how you said you didn't want to ride bareback so . . ." He went on to explain that since the young heroine in the movie was being chased by the two villains on their motorcycles, she wouldn't have time to put a saddle on her horse. The villains surprise her at her father's horse farm, so she'd have to get away from them very quickly. "So," he concluded, "it all fits in with the story very nicely, and my scriptwriters agree with me." He turned away from Whitney's angry face and spoke to Kerry. "You won't mind riding the scene again without a saddle, will you?"

Kerry smiled and shook her head. She'd ride it without a *bridle* if he asked her to!

"And what are you going to do when she falls off again?" Whitney retorted, her face white with fury.

He laughed. "This isn't a live play we're doing here. We'll just reshoot the scene till we get it right, that's all. So, Kerry Logan. What do you say? Do you want the part, or not?"

"Of course she does," Holly announced loudly.

Kerry just sat there, smiling foolishly, not daring to ask how long it would be before they would start the actual filming. Her shoulder was very sore and she hoped there would be enough time for it to heal properly before she and Magician had to go careening through the woods again.

Oblivious to Whitney's foul mood, Giles Ballantine told them that Kerry's ride would probably take place within seven to ten days. But, before that, he planned to bring the real star of the movie to the barn so he could shoot a couple of scenes with her and Magician, including one of her getting on his back. Then the rest of the scene belonged to Kerry.

"You mean she only got the part because she rode *bareback*?" Whitney said incredulously when he had finished.

"Just about," he replied. "And I really liked her horse, too. Black is a very dramatic color."

For an insane moment Kerry wondered if Whitney would offer to paint Astronaut black and tell Giles Ballantine how great she was at riding without a saddle.

"If I'd ridden bareback, would *I* have gotten the part instead of her?" Whitney persisted.

"Maybe." Mr. Ballantine got stiffly to his feet. As he was about to leave, Holly asked him one more question.

"Who's the star of the film?"

"Don't you know?" said Whitney, recovering her icy cool.

"It's Blair Hennessey," Giles said with a smile.

"*The* Blair Hennessey?" Holly choked out in an excited squeak. "The one who's in *Generations?*" she asked, naming one of her favorite TV shows.

The movie producer nodded and turned his attention to Whitney. "Don't forget to remind your mother that Blair will be staying at your house while we're shooting her scenes."

Whitney smiled triumphantly and started to gush. "Oh, it's going to be so much fun having Blair staying with me. I just know were going to hit it off. I've already made plans for a party at the country club, and a picnic and . . . I really have to go, I have so much to do!"

Then she sailed out of the office with her head in the air.

"I'm sorry I had to disappoint her," Giles Ballantine said in a slightly embarrassed voice, "especially after all the great hospitality Marion and Greg Myers have shown me. But it can't be helped. And I'm sure having a real movie star for a guest will help make up for it."

Kerry smiled at him. But even though Whitney had put on quite a show, Kerry still had the nagging feeling that Whitney wanted it all. She shuddered slightly and wondered what disaster Whitney could dream up that would put her in front of the camera instead of Kerry.

After Giles Ballantine left, Kerry and Holly walked back to the house. Kerry was grateful for the chance to rest her injured shoulder, but unfortunately, the week or so until filming also gave Whitney time to scheme her way back into the film. Kerry shook off the unpleasant thought. The strong-minded movie producer didn't strike her as someone that Whitney could wrap around her little finger the way she did with her parents.

Unless something awful happened to Magician or her, *she* and not Whitney would ride the scene through the woods. And after that she could start looking for her dream horse!

Chapter Six

"You'd better thank Whitney for the part," Holly said with a wicked grin just before they reached the back door.

Kerry looked at her in astonishment. "Why? After what she did with those prickers, I ought to string her up by her toes!"

"If she hadn't put those dumb prickers under your saddle, you'd never have ridden bareback, that's why."

Kerry grinned. "Poor Whitney! Her plan certainly backfired, didn't it?"

"Yeah," Holly said, opening the door. "And it's her own stupid fault. If she hadn't tried to sabotage your chances, Giles Ballantine might have chosen her instead."

"Too late now," Kerry said cheerfully, and she took a hard roll from the breadbin and started piling it high with lettuce, ham, and cheese. The morning's excitement had made her hungry, and her mouth started to water as she eyed her sandwich. "Hmmm, I bet she starts riding bareback now."

Holly burst out laughing, and then Liz poked her head around the door. "I guess it's good news, huh?"

Kerry nodded, her mouth full of sandwich.

"Well done," Liz said. "I'm very happy for you, Kerry, but I'm still worried about your shoulder."

"No problem," Kerry assured her. "They're not filming my scene for another ten days."

"Good." Liz poured herself a cup of coffee and sat down at the kitchen table. "Because I've got some news, too."

"What is it, Mom?"

"Do you remember Sally Fletcher, Holly?"

"Your old college roommate with the crazy family?"

Liz smiled. "I haven't seen her in almost five years, and she's just called. She's on her way to stay on the island and wants me to join her."

"What island?" Holly asked.

"Sally's family owns a whole island off the coast of Maine. I went there once, right after graduation, and it was really great. Crashing waves, enormous cliffs, and incredible white sand."

"Are you going to go, Mom?"

"Yes, as long as I won't miss Kerry's scene in the film."

Kerry explained Giles Ballantine's plans for the next ten days, including Blair Hennessey's arrival.

"That's perfect!" Liz exclaimed. "I can sneak off for a few days and get back in plenty of time. I really could use a break."

"And you deserve one, Mom."

"You sure do, Liz, but who's going to look after us?" Kerry asked.

Liz grinned. "You two don't really need looking after, but to set my mind at rest, I've asked Madge Parker to come up and keep an eye on things around here."

Holly squealed with delight. "Mom, that's great! I love Madge."

"Who's Madge?" Kerry asked.

"A very old friend who used to own a breeding farm," Liz replied. "She taught me to ride."

"Does she still have horses?"

"No, she sold the farm when her husband died. Now she writes books, instead."

"*Horse* stories?" Kerry asked, her curiosity aroused.

"Sometimes," Liz replied, "but I think she's into murder mysteries now." Then she got up. "I've got to call Sally back and tell her I'm coming, and firm everything up with Madge."

"You'll love Madge," Holly said happily. "She used to come and take care of me whenever Mom and Dad went away."

Madge Parker arrived two days later, complete with portable typewriter and an armload of half-finished manuscripts. She was a tall, rangy-looking woman with short, gray hair, a weatherbeaten face, and twinkling blue eyes. As soon as she caught sight of Holly standing on the front porch, she let out a loud yelp and dumped her typewriter right on the path. The manuscripts scattered across the front lawn, and as Kerry rushed to retrieve them, she could

59

hear Madge Parker exclaiming loudly over Holly's miraculous recovery.

Liz left at nine the next morning amid a flurry of last-minute instructions. She scribbled down the phone number where she could be reached and said, "Let's hope their phone system works."

"Come on, Mom, this *is* the twentieth century," Holly reminded her with a laugh.

"Hah! Not on *that* island, it isn't," Liz retorted. "They only got electricity out there a year ago, and the plumbing is positively antique!"

"Okay, kids, here's the routine," Madge said with a sparkle in her eye as soon as Liz had left the driveway. "You tell me how much help you need from me around the barn, and I'll pitch in. But don't expect me to cook. I'm the only person alive who can burn water, so I'm counting on *you* to feed me."

"Are you working on a new book?" Holly asked, eyeing the pile of manuscript on the kitchen table.

"You bet I am," Madge replied in a sinister voice. "And I'm at a crucial point, so I'm going to lock myself in your mother's office and try to figure out how to rescue my hero from the KGB! So, please don't have a crisis, okay?"

Holly assured her they weren't planning on one, and Kerry hoped she was right. It had been three days since Giles Ballantine told her she'd won the part over Whitney, and so far, nothing disastrous had happened. Her shoulder was getting better, and Magician was as fit as a fiddle. His sore had almost healed and Kerry knew she could ride him with a saddle, if she wanted to.

That afternoon, while Kerry was exercising Buccaneer in the outside riding ring, Whitney showed up with a pretty blond girl. Kerry realized at once it was Blair Hennessey. Since she didn't want to miss the expression on Holly's face when Blair walked into the barn, she left the ring and trotted toward the stables. "She's here!" she yelled to Holly as she led Buccaneer inside.

"Who?" Holly's voice sounded muffled.

"Blair Hennessey. Whitney's bringing her in now."

"Help!" Holly yelled, sticking her sweat-streaked face around Magician's stall door. "I can't meet her now! I'm a mess."

"Too late," Kerry murmured as Whitney and Blair entered the stables. "Don't worry, you look cute. Kind of like a barn rat."

Holly threw a curry comb at her and disappeared into the stall.

Kerry knew that unless she took the first step, Whitney would never bother to introduce her to the newcomer. As the pair walked down the aisle, she pushed herself in front of them and said, "Hi, I'm Kerry Logan, and Mr. Ballantine has asked me to help you with the horse."

Blair Hennessey smiled. She started to say something, but Whitney interrupted her rudely. "You don't have to bother with that today, Blair," she said in a silky voice. "Come on, I want to show you *my* horse."

"But," the young actress protested politely, "Giles wants me to get used to . . ." She paused, looking slightly embarrassed.

"You mean Magician?" Kerry prompted her.

"Yes, that's it," Blair said as she looked anxiously at the stalls on either side of her. "I'm a bit nervous around horses, and—"

Whitney cut her off again. "Come with me," she said. "You don't need Kerry. I can show you what he wants you to do."

Kerry shrugged and walked back into Magician's stall. "Whitney's really got her claws into Blair Hennessey," she said in a low whisper to Holly, who was still hiding behind her horse. "I doubt we'll be able to get anywhere near her."

Holly peeked out from behind her horse. "Where are they?"

"Looking at Astronaut." Then Kerry remembered that she'd forgotten to take Buccaneer's saddle and bridle off. "I'll be back in a minute," she said as she scurried out of Magician's stall and into Buccaneer's. It was directly across the aisle from Astronaut's stall, and she could hear quite clearly what Whitney was saying.

"Poor Kerry Logan." Whitney's voice had quite an authentic touch of sympathy to it. "She only works here, and I felt so sorry for her, I told Giles to go ahead and give her the part in the movie. She needs the money badly because her father's away. She's only staying with the Chapmans because she has nowhere else to go."

Kerry couldn't hear Blair's murmured reply because her own anger had started to boil. For a few seconds all she could hear was the sound of her heart, pounding loudly. Then Whitney spoke again. "He really wanted *me* to ride your part for you, Blair, but

63

I just couldn't help myself. I feel so sorry for Kerry. But don't tell him I told you that. Please. He doesn't want anyone to know he's soft-hearted enough to give the part to someone who isn't the best."

Kerry almost choked over Blair's innocent reply.

"Oh, Whitney, you're so generous. Kerry's lucky to have you for a friend."

Kerry stayed quietly in Buccaneer's stall until the two girls left the barn, and then burst furiously back into Magician's stall. "Did you hear that?" she exploded to an astonished Holly.

"Hear what?" asked Holly.

Kerry told her, and Holly started to giggle.

"It's not funny!" Kerry snapped.

"Oh come on, Kerry," Holly said softly. "You ought to be used to Whitney by now."

"But she doesn't have it in for you the way she does for me," Kerry growled.

"I know, but don't let her get to you. It doesn't matter what stupid stories she tells Blair Hennessey. The important thing is, you're riding in the scene, and she isn't."

"I guess you're right," Kerry admitted reluctantly. But Whitney's lies still upset her. How on earth was she going to work with the actress if Blair thought she was some poor kid that Giles Ballantine had taken pity on?

Madge looked upset when they got back to the house that evening. She was pacing around the kitchen with a frown on her face.

"What's wrong?" Holly asked.

65

"My stupid agent," Madge muttered angrily. "I may have to go to New York, darn it." She paused and stared at the two girls. "I'll try to straighten it out on the phone, but if I can't, will you two be okay on your own for a day?"

"Sure," Holly said cheerfully.

"But what about all this filming you're doing?" Madge asked.

Just as Kerry was about to say she wasn't really sure when she would be riding her scene, the phone rang. Holly picked it up, and then started to smile. "It's for you," she said, and handed the receiver to Kerry.

"Who is it?"

"Mr Ballantine," Holly replied in a loud whisper.

"Kerry," the movie producer's loud voice boomed down the phone lines. "I want you to be ready to start working with Blair, first thing tomorrow morning."

"What do you want me to do?"

Giles Ballantine chuckled. "The poor kid's really nervous about being around the horses. She's only ridden a couple of times before and she thinks she's going to fall off the minute she gets on Magician's back. Just spend some time making her feel at home . . . you know, teach her how to vault on his back the way you do. We'll be filming the scene just before your ride through the woods, and I need some good close-ups of Blair getting on the horse."

Kerry hung up feeling excited.

They were finally getting going on the project. When she went to bed that night, all she could think about was the horse she was going to buy with the five hundred dollars. In spite of Holly's doubts, Kerry

66

was sure she'd be able to find something. Not all horses cost as much as Susan Armstrong's, and she was confident she'd be able to find just what she wanted. In her imagination it would be a beautiful light bay, or maybe even a chestnut with a flaxen mane and tail, just like the horse in one of her favorite stories.

Chapter Seven

The film crew was already setting up their equipment when Kerry and Holly got to the barn early the next morning. They went straight to Magician's stall and, to their dismay, found out that he'd slept in a pile of manure. His coat was filthy, and his mane was all snarled up with pieces of dirty bedding.

"We'll have to give him a bath!" Holly wailed as she stared at her filthy horse.

"We'd better hurry," Kerry replied as she gathered up some empty buckets and the hosepipe. "Let's do this outside. He'll dry quicker in the sun."

They were rinsing him off when Blair Hennessey turned up. To Kerry's relief, there was no sign of Whitney. She gave Magician one last squirt with the hosepipe, and then Holly emerged from his other side to meet the famous actress. Poor Holly, she looked even worse than she had yesterday when she'd hidden in Magician's stall! Her hair was sopping wet, and she had streaks of dirt on her face and hands.

"Hi," Holly said shyly as Blair tentatively reached out to pat Magician on his nose.

"He's a pretty horse," the actress said admiringly.

Magician whinnied, and Blair quickly stepped away from him.

"He's mine," Holly said proudly as she wrapped her arms around Magician's soaking wet neck. "He's the best horse in the world."

Blair laughed daintily, showing off her perfectly straight, white teeth. As she moved her head, her long blond hair rippled and shimmered in the early morning sun.

Giles Ballantine interrupted any further conversation by his arrival, announcing loudly that Kerry and Blair were to start working with the horse. He wanted them ready to shoot by eleven o'clock.

"What do I have to do?" Blair asked nervously.

"Just get used to Magician," Kerry told her in a reassuring voice. "He's as gentle as a lamb. Look, why don't you walk beside me and we'll lead him around till he dries off. Then I'll show you how to vault onto his back."

Blair looked so horrified, that Kerry felt sorry for her. "Are you any good at gymnastics?" she asked shyly, hoping Blair had *some* athletic ability.

The actress nodded. "Yes, I am. It's one of the things I've had to learn, along with dancing, and singing . . ." She paused for a moment. "But not riding, I'm afraid. I've only been on a horse a few times."

"Don't worry," Kerry said confidently. "Nothing to it." She knew it was a huge lie, but Blair didn't have

69

to know. All she was going to have to do was get on Magician's back and sit there for a couple of seconds while the camera recorded her actions. And after that Kerry would be taking over.

As they walked slowly around the stable yard, being careful to stay in the full sun, Kerry found herself talking quite easily to the older girl. Blair told her she was sixteen, and had been acting since the age of seven.

The hot sunlight soon dried Magician's coat, and Kerry suggested that they start practicing. "I'll show you what to do." With one fluid movement Kerry vaulted onto Magician's back. "See, it's not hard," she said as she slipped off him.

"I can't do *that*," Blair wailed.

"Of course you can. Come on, Mr. Ballantine's watching us."

"Kerry, give her a leg up first, just so she can see what it feels like to sit on him," Holly suggested wisely.

"Good idea." Kerry pushed Blair up to Magician's side and told her to lift her left leg up a little. "That's it," she muttered encouragingly. "Now, hold on to his mane with your left hand, and when I shove you up, lean across his body and swing your right leg over his back."

Blair clenched her teeth and obediently lifted her leg.

Kerry bent down and hoisted Blair up and over Magician's back. Unfortunately, she misjudged it, and Blair disappeared in a flurry of arms and legs, landing with a loud thud on the other side.

Holly burst out laughing. Luckily, so did Blair.

"I'm sorry," Kerry blurted out as she blushed bright red. "I didn't realize you were so light. I'm used to helping Holly onto his back, and she weighs a ton!"

"I don't!" Holly yelled indignantly.

"Only teasing," Kerry muttered, hoping her attempt at a joke would encourage Blair to try again.

She did, and Kerry couldn't help but admire the girl's determination to succeed. After one more try, Kerry got her firmly installed on Magician's back. "See, it's not hard," she said cheerfully as she led the horse around slowly so Blair could get used to the feel of him.

"It's okay when you help me," Blair answered, but she still didn't sound convinced. "Look, if this doesn't work out, maybe Giles will agree to use *you* instead of me for this scene. All he has to do is make it a long shot instead of a close-up, and no one will know the difference. I'm going to be wearing a dark wig anyway. The character is supposed to have dark hair."

"Let's not give up yet," Kerry encouraged.

Blair got off Magician's back, and Kerry showed her how to vault onto his back without any help. "Just pretend he's a vaulting horse in a gym," she suggested helpfully.

"Great, but where are the handles?" Blair tried to joke.

"His mane will have to do."

After almost an hour of constant work, Blair was able to vault onto Magician's back on her own.

"I did it!" she yelled triumphantly.

"That's my girl," Giles Ballantine called out from where he was standing near the cameras. "You're

71

doing just great. Now, come on over here and get yourself into makeup. We've only got another half hour."

"How do you suppose we're going to get Magician to stand still while she gets on him?" Holly said as Blair walked toward the makeup table.

"Bribe him with a bag of carrots?"

"Be serious. Do you think she'll be able to hold his reins *and* vault onto his back at the same time."

"I hope so," Kerry muttered.

Whitney turned up just as Blair was finishing up with makeup. Kerry tried to ignore her as she substituted Magician's bridle for the halter that he had been wearing when they were only practicing. Then she showed Blair how to hold the reins, along with a chunk of mane, while she vaulted onto his back.

"Okay, everyone!" Giles Ballantine roared through his bullhorn. "This one's for real, now."

Kerry stood just out of the camera's range and watched nervously as a young man with a small blackboard ran in front of the camera. ACT 7, SCENE 1 was written on it in chalk, and as soon as he'd flipped the top of his clapperboard, the director yelled loudly, "Action!"

Almost immediately a hush fell over the crowd of people watching as Blair Hennessey made her first attempt to vault onto the horse's back. She almost made it, but Magician unfortunately stepped forward, and she fell off.

"Good try!" Giles boomed out encouragingly. "Let's try again."

Kerry felt sorry for Blair. She already looked hot

SCENE 7
TE 7/15   TAKE 3
ECTOR   CAM
BALLANTINE   ROLL 4

and miserable in the short, dark wig she was wearing for her scene, and small beads of sweat were starting to show through her heavy film makeup.

She tried again, with much more success, but Giles wasn't quite satisfied. However, he was very generous with his praise when the young actress got it right on the third try. "You're a terrific teacher, Kerry," he said happily after he'd told his astonished film crew that they had a successful take.

Kerry blushed. She grew even more embarrassed when Blair Hennessey threw her arms around her waist and gave her an enormous hug. "Thanks for being so patient with me," she said happily. "I never could have done this without your help."

"If looks could kill, you'd be dead," Holly whispered to Kerry urgently. "Look at Whitney. She thinks you're going to steal her latest 'best friend.'"

Kerry watched as Whitney ran up to Blair, took her arm possessively, and led her away from them as quickly as possible. Holly was right. She'd just given Whitney yet another reason to be jealous of her. Praise from Giles Ballantine for being a good teacher, plus Blair's unexpected show of affection.

As quickly as they'd set up, the production crew dismantled their equipment and loaded it into the huge trucks that were parked in the stable yard. Mr. Ballantine came up to Kerry before they took off and thanked her again for helping his young actress. "She was scared stiff, you know," he said warmly as he squeezed Kerry's hand. "Thanks for making it easy for her."

"No problem," Kerry muttered, and she rubbed

her sore shoulder without thinking. All that vaulting onto Magician's back had made it flare up again. She'd better ride that afternoon, just to make sure it didn't stiffen up on her.

After a quick lunch at the house, she asked Holly if she wanted to go with her on Buccaneer.

"No, but thanks," Holly replied. "I'm reading one of Madge's latest stories, and I want to finish it."

Kerry finished eating and ran back to the barn. She didn't mind riding on her own. In fact, she was looking forward to it—she and her horse alone on the trails. She brushed Magician quickly, and it didn't take long. He was still nice and clean from his bath. Then she ran into the tackroom for his saddle and bridle.

The only thing on Magician's peg was Holly's saddle. Kerry stared hard at it for a second or two, trying to remember what she'd done with his bridle when they'd finished filming that morning. She knew she'd hung it up where it belonged, but now it wasn't there. She hunted around the tackroom for another ten minutes, then gave up. Maybe Holly had put it somewhere else, so she ran back to the house to check with her.

"But can't you just borrow someone else's bridle?" Madge asked when Holly said she didn't know where it was.

"It's not the bridle that's the problem," Kerry explained quickly. "It's his *bit*."

"What about his bit?" Madge looked puzzled.

"Magician has to have a *vulcan* snaffle," Kerry told her. "His previous owners ruined his mouth with a twisted snaffle, and Magician has to have a soft, rubber bit."

"Barbarians!" Madge muttered angrily. "I hate people who don't know how to use severe bits on horses. They ought to be locked up."

"I know," Kerry wailed. "But what do I do now? I don't want to ride him in just a halter, especially on the cross-country course."

"Do you have a spare bridle, Holly?" Madge asked.

Holly nodded. "Yes, I've got a show bridle in my bedroom, but it's got a regular snaffle. Not the vulcan."

"Doesn't matter," Madge answered. "Now, all we need is some vet wrap, and I can fix up your snaffle. Magician won't know the difference."

"Can you really?" Kerry asked, feeling an enormous wave of relief.

"Nothing to it. Now, do you have any vet wrap?"

Kerry found a roll of the white, spongy stuff in one of the kitchen drawers, and Madge went to work, carefully wrapping the plain metal snaffle with a thick layer of the soft vet wrap. "There," she said proudly when she'd finished. "It'll work fine."

"Madge, you're a genius," Kerry said thankfully, and then ran back to the barn. As she tacked up the horse, she wondered what had happened to the other bridle. It couldn't have just walked out of the tackroom all by itself. Someone had to have taken it. Someone who knew about Magician's need for the special bit, and also someone who didn't want him being ridden!

Kerry knew she couldn't prove anything, but she was willing to bet her life that Whitney Myers had taken Magician's bridle. As she led the horse out of his stall, she saw Whitney's tack trunk beside Astronaut's stall door. Out of curiosity she lifted the lid and looked inside. Of course, it wasn't there, but she hadn't really expected it to be. Whitney might be a sneak, and a cheat, but she wasn't stupid. No, she'd have taken the bridle while Kerry was having lunch, and hidden it somewhere in her house. Then, when Kerry was unable to ride Magician because she didn't have the proper bit, Whitney would immediately get Giles Ballantine to use *her* and Astronaut instead.

Then Kerry saw the funny side of Whitney's pathetic attempt to get what she wanted. It was all so stupid. The girl was definitely getting desperate. Surely she ought to know that just stealing a bridle with a special bit wasn't going to stop Kerry from riding Magician in the film. A trip to their local tack shop for a new vulcan bit would solve the problem instantly, and besides, Madge's temporary fix with the vet wrap seemed to be working just fine. Magician was already contentedly mouthing his new bit, not seeming to mind at all.

As she rode off toward the cross-country course, Kerry hoped that this was all Whitney was capable of. If it was, then she had nothing to worry about. It was a stupid, futile attempt, and it hadn't worked.

The phone was ringing loudly when she got back to the house after her ride. It was for Madge.

"I guess I've got to go to New York after all," Madge said angrily when she'd finished her conversation. "I hate to go, and I'm rotten at getting up early. That miserable train leaves before the sun comes up!"

"Don't wake us up then," Holly teased affectionately. "And you're sure you'll be back tomorrow night?"

"You can count on it," Madge said firmly. "You won't catch me staying overnight in New York City!"

78

Chapter Eight

Kerry's shoulder was stiff and sore the next morning, and Holly generously offered to feed the horses by herself. As soon as she ran off to the barn, Kerry happily ran herself a tub full of hot water, looking forward to a long, leisurely soak in Liz's favorite bubble bath.

No sooner had she tested the steaming hot water with her toes than Holly burst through the bathroom door. "Magician! He's gone!" Holly shrieked.

Kerry stared at her in astonishment. "What do you mean, *gone*?"

"He's not in his stall," Holly wailed. "You didn't leave him out all night in one of the paddocks, did you?"

"Of course I didn't. I put him in his stall last night, fed the horses, and came back here."

"Well, he's not there now!" Holly cried. "Come on, Kerry, we've got to find him."

Kerry dressed in a flash and followed Holly over to the barn. "You didn't tell me his stall door was *shut*," Kerry said in horror when they reached Magician's empty stall. She stared at the closed door and looked at Holly's shocked expression.

"I didn't think about it," Holly said in a whisper.

"If his door *was* shut," Kerry said thoughtfully, "then he couldn't have gotten out by himself, could he? I mean, he wouldn't have shut it behind him when he escaped." She knew that this wasn't the first time Magician had managed to get out of his stall, and they always had to remember to fasten the bolt securely or else they'd find him wandering around loose somewhere.

Holly stared at her miserably. "Are you trying to tell me he didn't get out by himself? That he could have been *stolen*?"

"Unless one of the others got here before you did this morning, saw his open door, and shut it as they went by."

"I was the first one here," Holly said in a weak voice. "Sue and Robin turned up right after me. And none of the stall doors were open. I'd have noticed if they were. I didn't realize Magician was gone till I opened his door and went in to feed him." She put her hands over her face and started to cry.

"I'm going to call the police," Kerry said in a grim voice, wishing there were an adult around, instead of a bunch of kids.

"Maybe we ought to call Madge," Holly suggested as they went into Liz's office.

Kerry glanced at the clock on the wall. "No good,

80

Holly. She's still on the train to New York, and besides, how do we get in touch with her? We don't even know where she'll be."

Holly plopped herself down on the tack trunk while Kerry dialed the Winchester police station. Her misery only deepened as she listened to Kerry's end of the conversation. "What did they say?" she asked when Kerry put the phone down.

"They suggested we form a search party on horseback," Kerry said quietly. She wondered if she ought to tell Holly that the police officer had also told her that they'd had a few similar complaints in the past month. It seemed there was a string of horse thieves operating in New England, and already a few valuable horses were missing from other horse barns.

She decided to keep the information to herself. Holly didn't need any more bad news right now.

"I want to call Mom," Holly muttered unhappily.

"She can't help us right now," Kerry said gently. "She's *hours* away. It'd take her all day to get back here, and we'll have found him by then."

"You really think so?"

"You bet." Kerry knew she sounded more confident than she felt. "Let's get the others to help us. We'll all go out looking, and I bet you we find him before lunch."

Robin Lovell and Sue Armstrong agreed to help immediately. Then Kerry phoned Jennifer McKenna, and twenty minutes later she ran into the barn carrying her saddle.

"Who shall I ride?" Holly asked while the others were busy tacking up their horses.

Kerry hesitated. She *could* give Buccaneer to Holly, but he wasn't an easy horse to ride, especially out in the woods. If anything happened to Holly while she was riding him, Liz would kill both of them. "Do you want Buccaneer?" she offered hesitantly.

"No, I guess I'll stay here," Holly said sensibly. "One of us has got to be by a phone, anyway, in case someone calls to say they've found him."

Just as the four riders were about to leave the barn, Whitney showed up. For an awful, suspicious moment Kerry wondered if *she* had anything to do with Magician's sudden disappearance, but then she dismissed the thought immediately. Not even Whitney was mean enough to steal a horse!

"Where are you all going?" Whitney asked in a cool voice.

"Magician's lost," Robin said as she tried to calm her impatient horse. Tally Ho was raring to go, and already he was stamping his feet and tossing his head.

"Lost?" Whitney purred smoothly. "How did he get lost?"

"He got out of his stall," Kerry snapped angrily as she steered Buccaneer toward the barn door. "We're going out to look for him. We could use your help, too."

"Oh, I'm sorry," Whitney drawled in an apologetic voice, "but I promised Blair I'd watch them filming her scene in the village today. She's waiting for me now."

Kerry glared at her. As she walked her horse outside, she was angry enough to believe Whitney really *did* know something about Magician's disappearance.

83

"What are you going to do if you can't find him?" she heard Whitney's voice calling out to her from the barn. "Are you going to tell Mr. Ballantine he's gone?"

I'm sure you'll take care of *that*, Kerry thought bitterly as she swung her leg over Buccaneer's back. No doubt Whitney would take great pleasure in informing the movie producer that one of his "stars" was missing.

The four girls on horseback gathered together and tried to decide what to do. "Why don't Sue and I ride toward the village," Robin suggested helpfully. "There are a lot of open fields on the way, and I bet Magician's in one of them, stuffing his face!"

"Okay," Kerry said. She turned toward Jennifer. "And you and I can head up toward the ski area and check out the cross-country course."

"Yeah," Jennifer said with a grin. "Maybe Magician's already on the course, practicing for his big day."

Kerry smiled at the silly joke. But she wasn't smiling inside. That stall door had been shut when Holly had arrived in the barn, and horses that got out of their stalls didn't shut doors behind them. That left only one other explanation. He'd been *taken* out of his stall by someone, and that was something she didn't want to think about.

Robin and Sue rode off toward the village, and Kerry and Jennifer turned their horses toward the woods and trails that spread out below Timber Ridge Mountain.

"Do you think we'll find him?" Jennifer asked anxiously as they trotted along the wide trails that led to the Timber Ridge ski area.

"We've *got* to find him," Kerry answered her grimly. She knew that Holly's heart would be broken if her precious horse was never found. And on top of that, *she* wouldn't be able to ride in the film if Magician didn't turn up.

When they reached the meadow at the beginning of the cross-country course, Jennifer and Kerry decided to split up, figuring they could cover more ground if they were on their own.

While Jennifer rode Prince toward the cross-country course, Kerry cantered Buccaneer across the meadow. She squeezed through a break in the hedge and went into the next field. There were a few cows and a couple of ancient draft horses grazing there, but no sign of Holly's black horse.

"Magician! Magician!" Kerry called out over and over again as she trotted along. But there was no answering whinny. Only the echo of her own voice as it bounced off the mountain back at her.

By early afternoon she felt more miserable than ever. There was absolutely no sign of Magician, and she'd ridden for miles and miles, searching for him. Hoping that one of the others had had better luck, Kerry reluctantly turned around and headed back toward the barn. She looked at her watch. She had been out looking for over five hours, and even Buccaneer was exhausted. With his head drooping low on a loose rein, Kerry arrived at the barn at three o'clock. The others had already returned, and their horses were back in their stalls.

"Did anyone call?" Kerry asked hopefully.

"No. But I called the police again," Holly said in a tight voice. "Why didn't you tell me there've been horse thieves around here?"

"Because I didn't want to make you feel any worse than you already did," Kerry said gently to her best friend.

Holly burst into tears. "I'm going to call Mom," she said between sobs. "I know she can't do anything, but I'm really scared."

"Madge'll be back tonight," Kerry reminded her. "She'll know what to do."

"I hope so," Holly sniffed.

They tried three times to reach the number in Maine that Liz had given them, but each time they got the same result. An impersonal recording that told them in a monotone that the number was temporarily out of order.

"Mom said she didn't trust their stupid telephone!" Holly cried desperately when even the telephone supervisor had told them the same thing. "Now what do we do?"

Kerry had been thinking hard. Another of the many horse stories she'd read had just popped into her mind: one that she'd read a few years ago about a stolen horse.

"Let's try calling a few horse dealers," she said in a hopeful tone of voice. "We can give them Magician's description and tell them we think he's been stolen."

"You think it might work?"

"It's worth a try. Maybe whoever took him will try to sell him right away."

They spent the rest of the afternoon on the telephone, calling every horse dealer and horse auction in northern New England. Holly looked through all her horse magazines and wrote the phone numbers down for Kerry as she found them in the advertisements and the classified listings. Kerry called them all, but no one had seen or heard of Magician. One of them told her to keep on trying, though. "It's a bit too soon," he said sympathetically when Kerry had poured out their troubles to him. "Your horse hasn't been missing for twenty-four hours yet, so don't give up." He took her phone number and promised to call if he had any news.

Then they went back to the barn and fed the horses. Holly sniffed loudly when she looked at Magician's stall, and Kerry felt as if she had a lump of clay inside her stomach. At this point she didn't even care about the film. It wasn't important anymore. Only getting Magician back, safe and sound, was.

The telephone rang at eight o'clock, and for a moment neither of them moved.

"Do you think it might be . . ." Holly's voice trailed off as Kerry reached for the phone.

It was Madge, calling from New York. "I've gone and missed the last train," her voice came loudly through the receiver. "I'm afraid I'm going to have to stay here overnight and come back tomorrow morning. I'm sorry, but my meetings went on longer than I expected."

Kerry put her hand over the mouthpiece and told Holly what Madge had just said. "Shall I tell her?

Holly shook her head violently. "No, she can't do anything, and she'll only feel bad about leaving us alone. Tell her we're okay, and that we'll see her in the morning."

"Are you sure you kids will be okay without me for one night?" Madge insisted.

Kerry assured her they were fine, hoping silently that she wouldn't be struck dead for the lie she'd just told. But Holly was right. There wasn't anything Madge could do, any more than Liz could, and she was even farther away, stuck on an island with no telephone, somewhere off the coast of Maine.

Neither of them got much sleep that night. When Kerry woke up at five-thirty, it was still dark outside, and she couldn't go back to sleep. All she could think about was Magician, out there somewhere, lost or stolen, and probably scared to death.

Giles Ballantine and Tony Gibson turned up at the barn later that morning. "Whitney's just told me about your missing horse," he said in a gruff voice when he found Kerry and Holly in Liz's office.

Kerry nodded miserably. She didn't know what to say.

"I'm sorry about it," the movie producer continued, "and I know how worried you must be, but this gives *me* quite a problem as well."

Kerry knew what he was going to say. She'd been thinking the same thing herself ever since she'd gotten out of bed.

"I'm afraid that if the horse doesn't turn up by Friday, I'm going to have to use Whitney and her horse for the part."

"But you can't!" Holly blurted out frantically. "You've already shot a scene with Magician and Blair Hennessey."

"I'll just have to reshoot it with Blair and Whitney's horse," he told her sharply. And then his voice softened slightly. "Look, I'm really sorry, but there's not much I can do to help you. My film crew is already working on overtime to get the shooting done within our schedule, and I can't afford to release any of them to help you look for the horse. Are you sure you're doing everything you can?"

Kerry patiently told him of all their efforts so far, and he nodded approvingly. "Don't count on your local police for much help," he said when she had finished. "They probably couldn't care less about lost horses. They're too busy with other things."

Kerry knew he was right. The Winchester police had their hands full with the usual crowd of summer tourists that were in the area. They would be too busy unsnarling traffic jams to look for a misplaced horse.

Both Kerry and Holly felt slightly better when Madge finally got back from New York. She scolded them for not telling her about Magician on the phone the night before, and then she said, "I don't think he's been stolen!"

Holly looked at her hopefully. "Are you sure?"

"Magician wasn't the only valuable horse in the barn that night," Madge went on. "And if it was horse thieves, why would they have gone to all that trouble for only one horse? Wouldn't they have taken some of the others as well?"

Kerry gasped in astonishment. She hadn't thought of it that way. But of course, Madge was absolutely right. Buccaneer, Astronaut, Tara, Prince, and Tally Ho were all valuable horses. Why would a horse thief just take Magician and leave the others behind?

She started to feel a lot better. Maybe Magician hadn't been stolen after all. And when Holly started to smile as she told Madge how good Magician was at getting out of his stall, Kerry knew they were going to find him.

But if she wanted to find him in time for her riding scene in the film, they were going to have to work fast. Friday was only two days away. If they hadn't found the missing horse by then, Whitney and Astronaut would get the part instead!

Chapter Nine

Madge took charge of the missing-horse operation with the efficiency of a marine drill sergeant! Kerry and Holly scuttled about the house in a frenzy as Madge barked orders at them. One of those orders was to round up all the local area maps they could lay their hands on.

"But what *kind* of maps?" Holly asked.

"Hiking trail maps, town road maps, and a trail map of your local ski area, if you can find one," Madge said as she organized the piles of papers that were spread out over the Chapmans' kitchen table.

While Holly went off to search for the maps, Madge had Kerry make a list of all the local 4-H groups and Pony Clubs. Madge planned to call all of them in her effort to gather together her team of horses and riders who would start looking for Magician early the next morning.

"Tell them to be here by nine," Madge said to Kerry

when the list was complete.

"But we've already gone out on horseback looking for Magician," Kerry reminded her politely.

"Hah! That was only four of you," Madge replied with a smile. "Now get busy. I want at least two dozen horses and riders. We've hundreds of acres to cover, and we haven't got a minute to lose."

Madge's expert organization produced twenty-five eager volunteers on horseback, including Robin, Sue, and Jennifer. Even Holly was going this time, riding Pumpkin, the fat little chestnut pony that all the beginner kids learned to ride on.

When all the horses and riders were assembled in the outside riding ring, Madge strode around like a sergeant major in charge of her troops. She broke them up into teams of three, then gave each group a map of the area they were to search. She'd spent hours the night before, drawing detailed maps of the whole area, marking roads, trails, farms, and land-marks so the searchers wouldn't get lost or cover the same ground as another team.

Kerry found herself the odd one out and decided she'd be more effective if she rode on her own. Buc-caneer was much faster than the horses in Holly's group, and she set off with Madge's map that cov-ered the wilderness on the other side of Timber Ridge Mountain.

As she rode down the trail, Kerry adjusted the old halter she'd put on Buccaneer's head over his bridle, and checked to make sure she had enough carrots with her. Magician wasn't always an easy horse to catch. So along with the halters, each team of riders had been issued a generous supply of Magician's favorite snack!

Kerry smiled to herself as she rode along the logging trail that wound its way around the eastern side of Timber Ridge Mountain toward her designated search area. Madge was quite incredible: she hadn't missed a single detail. She'd organized the whole search operation brilliantly, right down to the halters and carrots.

After about an hour on the same trail, she checked Madge's map. There was a fork in the trail up ahead, and she had to keep left. The other one led back to the village. The dirt-covered trail got wider after the fork, and pretty soon Kerry realized she was on one of the ski trails. Every few hundred yards other trails branched off through the woods. They all had small, wooden signposts bearing odd-sounding names like Jaws of Death, and Devil's Leap.

Kerry grimaced. If *she* ever took up skiing, she'd be sure and stay far away from trails with names like that.

She continued uphill for another half mile, and then the trail suddenly started to descend. It got so steep, she had to lean back on Buccaneer's rump to help him balance himself as he picked his way carefully down the rocky hillside.

When the trail finally leveled off, Kerry could see a small, ramshackle building underneath a clump of trees in the distance. At first she thought the strange-looking house was deserted, but then she saw smoke curling upward out of its old chimney.

The house wasn't much more than a two-room

shack, and it was incredibly old and in bad need of repair. The chimney was cracked and tilted crazily to one side. There were a couple of large holes in the roof, and what paint had once been on the clapboard siding was now hanging off in shreds.

As she sat on her horse trying to summon up the courage to approach the dilapidated little shack, the front door opened and an old man staggered onto the porch. He was wearing baggy, stained sweatpants and a filthy sweatshirt. And even from where Kerry was sitting, she could tell he hadn't shaved in weeks. A dark shadow of stubble covered the lower half of his face, and in his right hand he was clutching a can.

Great! she muttered to herself, and urged Buccaneer past the house as fast as she could. I guess I've just found the town bum, and there's no way I'm going to ask him if he's seen Magician.

As Buccaneer broke into a trot, Kerry could hear the old man shouting at her. She didn't look back. His words were slurred and impossible to understand, and she guessed he was yelling at her for trespassing. She slowed her horse down to a walk after they'd rounded the next corner. Then she looked back. She could still see the shack through the trees, but there was no sign of its owner. She heaved a sigh of relief and looked at her watch. Eleven forty-five. She'd been gone almost three hours, and just as she was wondering if any of the other search teams had had any luck, Buccaneer let out a loud neigh.

Kerry's heart almost jumped out of her mouth. Could it be? Was he calling to his old stable mate?

94

Buccaneer's ears were pricked forward, and he was now whinnying softly.

And then she saw why. Her hopes sank when she spotted the thin, scruffy-looking horse that had just walked out of an old shed in the field beside the trail. She glanced back toward the old man's shack and wondered if he could possibly be the owner of the pathetic animal.

Buccaneer squealed once and cautiously stuck his nose over the fence toward the strange horse. Kerry looked at it closely. Underneath all the mud and caked-on dirt, she guessed it was a chestnut. Its mane and tail were hopelessly tangled with bits of twigs and prickers, and it was impossible to tell what color was under all the dirt and grime.

Kerry slid off Buccaneer's back and tied him to the fence. Then she pulled a couple of carrots out of her pocket. The poor horse looked as if it hadn't had anything decent to eat in ages. As the animal timidly sniffed the carrot in her outstretched hand and took the treat, Kerry caught a glimpse of its teeth. She was quite surprised. They didn't look like the teeth of an old horse, and yet the animal, with its prominent withers and visible ribs, looked at least fifteen years old.

She was so busy examining the chestnut horse that she failed to notice another horse coming out of the shed. It wasn't until she got nudged firmly in the shoulder that she looked up.

"Magician!" Kerry shrieked. "I don't believe it! I've found you." She flung her arms around his neck and buried her head in his tangled mane. "What are you

doing here?" she cried. And then she quickly ran her hands over his neck and shoulders, looking for any sign of injury. But apart from being streaked with mud, he was in perfect health. Kerry sighed with relief and shook her head. Thank goodness she'd found him.

Magician whinnied happily and nuzzled her hand, looking for carrots. "You greedy old thing," Kerry said affectionately, and reached into her pocket for his treat.

"I've got to get you out of here," Kerry said quickly as Magician munched on the carrots. She hoped the old man couldn't see her from his house. She looked around for a gate. The only one she could see led directly into the man's back yard, and there was no way she was going to use that.

She stared at the wooden fence. It wasn't very high, and it was the only way out. Quickly she took the halter off Buccaneer's head and slipped it onto Magician. Then, without hesitating, she vaulted onto his back and trotted him toward the center of the field. She wheeled him around and dug her heels into his sides. In a flash he cantered forward and leaped over the old wooden fence, landing safely on the other side.

She quickly scrambled off his back, untied Buccaneer, and swung herself into his saddle. With Magician's lead rope firmly in her right hand, she started to ride back the way she had come. The chestnut mare whinnied pitifully. Kerry hated leaving the poor thing in that awful place, but she had no choice. She had to get back to the barn!

With her heart thumping away loudly inside her, Kerry walked the horses quietly by the old man's shack. Just when she thought she was safe, he lurched out onto the front porch.

"Where d'ya think you're goin'?" he yelled. "Come back! You can't take my horse!"

Kerry didn't wait to argue with him. "Let's go!" she shrieked at the top of her voice, but Buccaneer didn't respond quickly enough. The old man stumbled across his front yard and snatched at her horse's bridle.

"You're a thief!" he screamed at her as his bony hands clutched Buccaneer's reins.

Kerry bit her lip and kicked Buccaneer as hard as she could. Then she swung the end of Magician's lead rope at the old man's head. "Go away!" she yelled as the rope swished by his face. "Let me go!"

The old man tried to duck out of her way, but he wouldn't let go of Buccaneer's reins. Kerry desperately tried to pull them out of his grasp, but he was too strong for her.

"That's my horse!" he cried in a whining voice. And he made a grab for Kerry's leg. She kicked Buccaneer hard, and the big horse swung sideways, knocking into the old man. He fell away from the horse and let go of the reins.

Kerry saw her opportunity to escape. She kicked the horse again, and he took off up the path with Magician beside him.

"Come back! Come back!" the old man screamed angrily.

Kerry didn't look back. She wanted to put as much distance between her and that awful old man as she could. She galloped to the top of the hill and didn't slow down until she was riding down the other side. There was no way that old man could catch them now, not even if he came after them in his beat-up old truck.

Her return journey took an hour longer than her solitary ride on Buccaneer that morning. She couldn't go nearly as fast, leading another horse beside her, and it was four o'clock before she reached the stables.

Holly was the first one to spot her. "Where did you find him?" Holly cried with tears in her eyes. She flung her arms around Magician's neck and hugged him. "You're back, you're not lost anymore."

Shouts of welcome and cheers drowned out Kerry's mumbled reply. She was suddenly exhausted and her shoulder had started to ache.

Madge bustled out of the barn with a broad smile of satisfaction on her face. "Want a hamburger?" she asked Kerry.

"Did *you* cook it?" Kerry asked with a grin. She hadn't forgotten what Madge had told them about her failure as a cook.

"No," Holly interrupted. "Mom did." As Kerry slowly peeled her aching body off Buccaneer's saddle, Holly told her that her mother had arrived back at the barn at lunchtime. After Madge had explained what was going on, Liz had promptly brought her barbecue grill over to the barn and had started to cook hot dogs and hamburgers to feed the crowd of starving riders as they returned from their search.

"Am I the last one back?" Kerry mumbled as she bit into her hamburger.

"Yes," Liz answered with a smile. "And thank you for finding Magician, Kerry. You've no idea how upset Holly was when I got home."

Just then Whitney and Blair Hennessey drove up in Mrs. Myers's car. Blair jumped out immediately and ran over to the happy group of people clustered around Magician and Kerry. Kerry smiled at her and then glanced toward the car. Whitney was standing beside it, her face registering a mixture of horror and disappointment. And no wonder. Magician's return had completely wiped out any chance she had of riding in Giles Ballantine's movie.

Chapter Ten

"I still don't understand how you knew Magician hadn't been stolen," Liz said to Madge after supper that night.

The mystery writer smiled. "While everyone was out looking for the horse, I decided to test my theory."

"What theory?" Holly asked, her eyes opening wide.

"About that stall door. You said it was shut when you got to the barn and found Magician was missing, right?"

Holly nodded. "Yeah, and there's no way a horse can shut a stall door after it."

Madge continued, her eyes twinkling merrily. "I went into the barn, opened Magician's door, and left it. About ten minutes later it swung shut. All by itself. I knew then everyone had jumped to the wrong conclusion. You see, when you saw that the door was shut, you assumed that someone had taken the horse and shut the door behind them. But that door swung shut all by itself, and when you add that to the fact that none of the other horses were stolen, it proves Magician escaped all by himself."

"Well, he won't get out again," Liz said, "because we've put a padlock on his door. That ought to stop his thirst for adventure!" She grinned at her daughter. "Boy, am I glad to be home. The island was great, but with the phones out of order and the plumbing making noises in the night, I don't think I want to go back in a hurry. Besides, I missed too much!"

Madge announced she was ready for bed, and Liz decided that she was, too. As soon as the two adults disappeared, Holly asked Kerry to tell her more about how and where she'd found Magician.

Kerry repeated the bizarre story one more time. "But what I can't figure out is why an old man like that would own a horse," she finished.

"You don't suppose he *stole* her, do you?" Holly asked.

Kerry shrugged. "He probably did. I mean, he yelled at me when I took Magician away, and called him his horse. I bet he found Magician wandering around by his house and locked him up in the field."

"Magician could have jumped out and come home," Holly said with a grin.

"Uh-uh," Kerry replied. "I think he liked that little chestnut horse too much. You should have seen the way he was nuzzling its mane."

"Was it a mare or a gelding?"

"A mare," Kerry said. "Poor thing. I felt awful leaving her behind."

"Maybe the old man was going to *eat* it!" Holly cried

suddenly. "People do eat horses, you know."

"Yuch!" Kerry exploded. "That's gross!" Then she yawned. She was too tired to stay awake any longer. As she got ready for bed, her thoughts kept returning to the chestnut horse in the old man's field. She couldn't get the pathetic creature out of her mind, and she resolved to go back and take another look at her as soon as the filming was over.

By eight the next morning the film production crew had arrived at the barn. They only had one more day to prepare for Kerry's riding scene, and there was still a great deal to be done. One of the huge trucks had two large Harley-Davidson motorcycles in it. When they were wheeled out, Kerry led Magician over so he could check them out. She hoped he wouldn't freak out completely when they were riding in the woods, and both motorcycles were chasing them over the jumps.

Giles Ballantine saw her introducing the horse to his mechanical co-stars, and he came up to talk to her. "Thank goodness you found him," he said, patting Magician's neck as the black horse sniffed warily at the motorcycles. "I really didn't want to have to reshoot Blair's scene over again with Whitney's horse. I like this one much better."

Kerry asked him who was going to be riding the motorcycles.

"A couple of stuntmen. They'll be here soon, and I want them to run the course a few times before tomorrow."

The movie producer then explained some of the technicalities involved in shooting the tricky scene.

For the most part they would shoot the horse and rider and the motorcycles separately, then splice them together during film editing.

"So they really *won't* be chasing me, then?" Kerry said, feeling very relieved. The motorcycles were quite enormous and she knew they'd make a terrible noise.

"Only over *one* of the jumps," Mr. Ballantine said. "I want a wide-angle shot of you in front, with the bikes behind, and I'm afraid we can't achieve that with camera tricks. You, *and* the bikes, will have to jump the Tiger's Trap together."

Ugh, Kerry thought to herself. Trust Giles Ballantine to choose the most difficult jump. She asked how the bikes were going to get over it.

"We'll put a small wooden ramp over to one side for the bikes so they'll be able to clear the jump," he said. "It won't be in your way, and since the camera's on the far side of the jump, the audience won't see it."

"But that's not . . ." Kerry groped for the right word. ". . . *real*!" she finally blurted out.

Giles Ballantine roared with laughter. "But very dramatic, though, you must admit."

Then he excused himself and took off in a hurry to greet the two stuntmen, who'd just driven up in a flashy-looking red sportscar.

The taller of the two stuntmen introduced himself to Kerry as Mark Winters. "Why don't my brother, Matt, and I get our bikes going so you and your little horse here can kind of get used to them." He waved to the other stuntman, who was still by the car, talking to Mr. Ballantine.

Kerry thought it sounded like a good idea. She vaulted onto Magician's back, and ten minutes later both motorcycles and the horse and rider were chasing one another around the outside riding ring. At first Mark and Matt Winters stayed well away from her, with their throttles turned down low. But as Magician got more comfortable being around the noisy machines, they edged closer.

By the time the trio of riders had finished racing around the ring, Kerry felt much more confident about the next day's filming. Magician seemed to be getting used to the noisy machines.

The next morning Kerry and Holly arrived at the start of the cross-country course early. It seemed as if almost everyone from Timber Ridge had gathered there, too, to watch the exciting event. Everyone except Whitney Myers. And for that, Kerry was grateful. Whitney's possible appearance during the filming was the only thing that had been worrying her. So when Robin told her that Whitney's mother had taken her to New York for the weekend, she heaved a sigh of relief.

"Aren't you excited?" Jennifer asked as Kerry helped herself to a sticky doughnut and a carton of orange juice from the refreshment table.

Kerry nodded. "And I'm scared stiff as well," she joked through a mouthful of crumbs.

Holly sat down on the grass and started sorting through her knapsack. "Ah, here it is." She held up a can of hair spray.

"What's *that* for?" Kerry asked. She grinned, wondering if all the glamour of the occasion had gone to her friend's head and if Holly had decided to fix her hair.

"For you!"

Kerry instinctively reached up and felt her hair. The last time she'd looked at it in the bathroom mirror that morning, it had been fine.

Holly giggled. "I'm going to spray Magician's back . . . where you sit," she explained to a bewildered Kerry. "It'll make him all sticky. So you won't slide off him."

Kerry stared at Holly as though she'd lost her mind. But Liz said she thought it sounded like it might help. So Kelly shrugged and said she'd try it.

"Come and get your makeup on, Kerry!" a voice suddenly yelled in her ear.

Kerry whirled around in surprise. She hadn't expected *that*. "Do I *have* to?" she complained to Tony Gibson as he took her by the arm.

"If you don't wear makeup," he explained patiently, leading her toward the tent where the makeup and wardrobe people were waiting, "the camera will make your face look as white as a sheet." And then he chuckled. "We do want you to look kind of scared while you're being chased, but Giles will have a fit if you come off looking like a ghost!"

Twenty minutes later Kerry looked at herself in the mirror and gasped. She hardly recognized herself. Her face was covered with thick, greasy pancake that made her look as if she'd just spent three years in the tropics. She peered closer at her strange image. There was eyeshadow and mascara on her eyes, and a healthy dose of blusher on her cheeks. When she tried to smile, it felt as if all the makeup was going to crack and fall off her face. And last, but not least, the makeup artist positioned a short, dark wig on her head. Kerry barely recognized herself.

"Come on," Tony Gibson said as he handed her a pale blue silk shirt. "Put this on, and you're all set."

Kerry recognized the shirt as the same one that Blair Hennessey had worn for her scene when she'd vaulted onto Magician's back four days before. "What about these?" Kerry asked, pulling at her jeans.

"They're fine. They look like the ones Blair was wearing, and the camera won't be close enough to pick up any small differences."

Finally she was ready. She went outside the tent and took Magician's reins from Holly. He was wearing his show bridle with the temporary bit, and Kerry idly wondered if his other one would miraculously show up once the filming was over. She just knew Whitney had taken it, and she figured that the sneaky girl would probably just leave it somewhere in the barn one day when no one was looking.

Mr. Ballantine came up and told her that the first scene would be her, on Magician, cantering out of the woods and across the meadow toward the first cross-country jump. The two stuntmen on their motorcycles were already waiting in position, and Kerry trotted up to join them.

Mark and Matt Winters waved at her and revved their engines. Magician twitched his ears once or twice, then he ignored the noisy machines. Kerry gripped him firmly with her legs and forced her mind clear of everything except the scene.

As soon as the camera was pointed in her direction, all her nervousness disappeared. She began to feel like a real movie star. As she galloped across the meadow with the Harley-Davidsons following her, Kerry felt like shouting with joy. This was fun, and on top of it all, she was getting paid for it!

"Look like you're scared!" Giles Ballantine yelled through his bullhorn as Kerry and Magician cantered into the woods. "You're being chased by bad guys!"

Kerry fought down a grin and tried to look frightened. She leaned forward into Magician's flying mane and urged him to lengthen his stride. The bikes were close behind, and ahead she could see another camera, capturing her mad dash through the woods.

Ahead of her was the Tiger's Trap jump, and in front of it a small wooden ramp for the motorcycles. She trotted Magician up to it so he could get a good look at the ramp before he had to jump.

As soon as Giles had everything ready, he yelled for action. Kerry gathered up her reins and started to canter down the path toward the jump. Trees and spectators became a fuzzy blur as she picked up speed.

As Magician gathered himself up for the takeoff, Kerry almost forgot she was acting. With the roar of the two motorcycles ringing in her ears, she really felt as if she were riding for her life.

As soon as Magician landed safely on the other side of the jump, Kerry risked a quick glance back over her shoulder. The two Harley-Davidsons were soaring over the Tiger's Trap behind her. For a few sec-

onds their engines screamed at a different pitch while they were suspended in midair, and then they both hit the ground hard, and bounced.

"It's a take!" Giles Ballantine roared. With a mighty effort, Kerry pulled Magician down to a walk. His sides were heaving with exertion, and Kerry could feel beads of sweat erupting on her face through the heavy makeup.

"Well done!" Liz and Holly yelled out.

"That was great, Kerry!" Blair Hennessey cried.

Kerry rode up to them and slid off Magician's back. It was all over, and from the smile on the movie producer's face, she knew she'd done well.

"Fantastic ride," he said as he clapped her heartily on her back. "That's going to look spectacular on film."

Everyone crowded around, congratulating her. Giles told her that he'd send her check over the next day. Kerry thanked him. Now she could finally think about the horse she was going to buy! Images of bright chestnuts and gleaming bays shot through her mind all the way back to the barn.

But as she brushed the sweat off Magician's coat, one particular image kept returning to haunt her. It was the poor little chestnut horse in the old man's field. She couldn't get the animal out of her mind. She knew she had to go back and see it again.

Chapter Eleven

A feeling of anti-climax washed over Kerry when she woke up the next morning. Liz was taking Holly to the clinic for a checkup, and after they left, Kerry wandered around the house feeling strangely detached. All the fuss and excitement of the filming was over, and by the end of the day she'd have her check for five hundred dollars. She knew she ought to feel excited about earning all that money, but all she could think about was the poor, pathetic little chestnut mare in the old man's field. She just couldn't get the mistreated creature out of her mind.

She put down the horse magazine she'd been reading, and decided to risk a trip to the other side of Timber Ridge Mountain. Maybe the disgusting old man wouldn't be there. Quickly, she pulled on her riding boots and headed toward the barn. From the empty stalls, she guessed that Sue, Jennifer, and Robin had gone trail riding.

Magician and Buccaneer both whinnied happily when she approached their stalls. She fed Buccaneer a handful of M&Ms, and slipped Magician a large carrot. "Okay," she said with a grin, "which one of you wants to go trail riding?"

Buccaneer put his ears forward and looked at her quizzically.

Kerry laughed, and rubbed his nose. "You win," she said fondly. Quickly, she ran a brush over his gleaming, mahogany-colored coat, and idly wondered how long it would be before his owner took him away. She'd really miss the candy-loving horse when he went to Giles Ballantine's farm in Pennsylvania. Thinking about Buccaneer's departure from Timber Ridge reminded Kerry that once he left, she wouldn't have a horse to ride. All the more reason to hurry over to the old man's field and take another look at the chestnut mare. Maybe she was only kidding herself that she could rescue the animal and restore it to good health.

Magician neighed loudly when she left the barn with Buccaneer, and Kerry felt a twinge of guilt at leaving him behind.

Buccaneer was full of high spirits and wanted to race. It only took Kerry an hour to get to the old man's tumbledown shack. As she cautiously approached the tiny building, she crossed her fingers and hoped the owner wasn't around.

Luck was with her! No one came out onto the front porch as she trotted by on Buccaneer. Kerry heaved a sigh of relief when she was finally past the shack, and in sight of the old man's field.

There was no sign of the chestnut mare, and Kerry's heart gave a lurch. Maybe the old man had sold her, or worse . . . She shuddered, remembering what Holly had said about some people eating horses!

Buccaneer started to whinny softly. "What is it, boy?" Kerry murmured. Just then, she caught sight of the chestnut mare, walking stiffly toward them. She'd been hidden in the shade of a clump of trees in the far corner of the field.

"Come on, girl," Kerry called out. She jumped off Buccaneer's back and slipped his reins over her arm.

Slowly and timidly, the chestnut mare approached the fence. Kerry leaned over, and coaxed the mare toward her with a handful of carrots.

As the half-starved animal gobbled down the treats, Kerry slipped through the fence, and ran her hand over the mare's back and felt her bony ribs and withers. Chunks of dead hair fell away, and she could see signs of lice. She shuddered, and then grew angry. The old man deserved to be shot for keeping a horse in this condition.

Then she tried to study the animal objectively. Could she possibly perform a miracle and transform this thin, scrawny-looking bag of bones into a sleek, well-nourished horse? She shook her head, not knowing what to think. Maybe it was too far gone.

As she stared at the mare's fine-boned head and large, sad-looking brown eyes, she knew Liz would tell her she was crazy for even thinking she could rehabilitate this horse. And what about the others? Whitney, for instance? She'd never stop laughing if Kerry brought this horse into the barn. Even Holly